I'm Att...

the famous

I don't know abou... ...s a
good party, especially at Christmas time.
Find out what happens when I go to
Scotland for a traditional Hogmanay with
the Cheddar family. I can promise you,
there is a mystery in store.

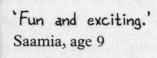

'Fun and exciting.'
Saamia, age 9

'Atticus is naughty and
really cool!'
Lucas, age 7

'Atticus Claw is fantastic.'
Charlotte, age 8

As you probably guessed from the picture, Atticus closely resembles me! I mean me, Henry the cat, not me, Jennifer Gray, the author. I'm thrilled to have so many fans and wanted to let you know that my, I mean, Atticus's new adventure is even funnier and more exciting than the last one. Thanks, Jennifer, for turning me into an action-cat hero! And thanks, you guys, for reading.

Henry (and Jennifer)

ATTICUS CLAW

Jennifer Gray is a barrister, so she knows how to spot a cat burglar when she sees one, especially when he's a large tabby with a chewed ear and a handkerchief round his neck that says Atticus Claw. Jennifer's other books include *Guinea Pigs Online*, a comedy series co-written with Amanda Swift and published by Quercus, and *Chicken Mission*, her latest series for Faber. Jennifer lives in London and Scotland with her husband and four children, and, of course, Henry, a friendly but enigmatic cat.

By the same author

ATTICUS CLAW
Breaks the Law

ATTICUS CLAW
Settles a Score

ATTICUS CLAW
Lends a Paw

ATTICUS CLAW
Goes Ashore

ATTICUS CLAW
Learns to Draw

JENNIFER GRAY

'ATTICUS CLAW'
on the Misty Moor

ff

FABER & FABER

First published in 2015
by Faber and Faber Limited
Bloomsbury House, 74–77 Great Russell Street,
London WC1B 3DA

Designed and typeset by Crow Books
Printed in England by CPI Group (UK) Ltd, Croydon, CR0 4YY

A CIP record for this book
is available from the British Library

ISBN 978–0–571–31710–3

FSC
www.fsc.org
MIX
Paper from
responsible sources
FSC® C101712

4 6 8 10 9 7 5 3

For George
with special thanks to Henry

It was Christmas Day and Atticus Grammaticus Cattypuss Claw, once the world's greatest cat burglar and now its best-ever police cat, was relaxing on Inspector Cheddar's favourite armchair at number 2 Blossom Crescent, Littleton-on-Sea. Atticus had just finished his Christmas lunch and his tummy was pleasantly full of turkey.

'That was delicious,' Callie said, throwing herself on the sofa.

'Really good,' Michael agreed, sprawling on the rug in front of the Christmas tree, 'especially the roast potatoes and gravy.'

Mrs Cheddar joined them. 'Yes, thank you, darling,' she called to her husband. 'It was even better than last year.'

'You're welcome.' Inspector Cheddar's cheery voice came from the kitchen as he went about collecting plates and stacking them in the dishwasher. Inspector Cheddar always did the cooking on Christmas Day. It was a Cheddar family tradition. 'Do you want pudding now or shall we open our presents first?' he asked.

'Presents first,' the children chorused.

'I thought you'd say that!' Inspector Cheddar said amiably.

Presents after lunch was another Cheddar Christmas family tradition.

Inspector Cheddar came into the sitting room and rearranged Atticus so that there was room for both of them in the armchair.

Atticus wished every day could be like Christmas. Normally Inspector Cheddar just booted him off.

There was a big pile of presents under the

Christmas tree. Michael sat on his heels and started handing them out.

'One at a time,' Inspector Cheddar said. 'And remember to fold the paper so we can use it again next Christmas.'

'You always say that, Dad!' Michael rolled his eyes at Callie. Callie giggled.

Atticus understood why. Inspector Cheddar got so excited about Christmas presents he never took his own advice. He couldn't wait for his turn to open a present and he always ripped the wrapping paper to shreds as soon as he got his hands on one.

'Mum can start!' Michael handed a gift to Mrs Cheddar. 'This is for you, Mum, from me and Callie.'

Mrs Cheddar peeled off the Sellotape carefully.

'Hurry up!' Inspector Cheddar said.

'I'm trying not to tear the paper,' Mrs Cheddar protested. 'You said you wanted to keep it for next year!' She winked at the children.

'I didn't say take all day about it, though, did I?' Inspector Cheddar said impatiently. 'Pass me a present, Michael. It'll be next Christmas before Mum opens that one at the rate she's going.'

Michael handed Inspector Cheddar a parcel. Inspector Cheddar grabbed it and ripped it open with his thumbs.

'Well, if you're going to be like that . . .' Mrs Cheddar laughed.

After that everyone dived in, including Atticus. Very soon the rug was piled high with a mountain of torn Christmas paper.

'Phew, that was fun!' Michael said when all the presents had been unwrapped.

'I told you we should have folded up the paper,' Inspector Cheddar grumbled. 'Look at the mess!'

Callie and Michael laughed. 'Honestly, Dad!' said Callie. 'You made most of it.'

'I'll go and get a bin bag,' Mrs Cheddar offered.

Atticus inspected his presents while Mrs Cheddar pushed the remnants of the wrapping paper into a recycling sack.

'Thanks, Mum, thanks, Dad, thanks, Atticus,' said Callie. 'I love all my presents.'

'So do I,' said Michael.

Michael had a new games console and Callie, who loved dressing up, had a new doctor's outfit. They also had books, DVDs, sweets, toys, and, from Atticus (who was good at paw prints), special Christmas cards that he had made with Mrs Cheddar's help.

'I love my presents too,' said Mrs Cheddar. 'They're very thoughtful.' Mrs Cheddar was keen on gardening. Inspector Cheddar had given her a new pair of wellington boots and two books, which were entitled *How to Make Compost* and *How to Grow Your Own Veg*. She also received some homemade fudge from the children, and a new hairbrush from Atticus to replace the one the children had borrowed to brush his brown-and-black-striped fur and four white socks.

'What about you, Atticus?' Michael asked. 'Do you like your presents?'

Atticus purred throatily. Of course he did! He had a stocking full of cat treats from Callie and Michael, some Thumpers' Badge Bright for his police-cat-sergeant badge from Inspector Cheddar and a new red handkerchief embroidered with his name on it from Mrs Cheddar. 'For when the other one gets dirty,' she said.

Atticus always wore a handkerchief with his name on around his neck. A spare one would be very handy.

'And I like mine too,' said Inspector Cheddar. Atticus had given Inspector Cheddar a sticky roller for removing cat hair from his uniform, and he had a new notebook and pen from the

children for writing down important things when he was investigating a crime. 'Although I'm not sure what this one is,' he added. Mrs Cheddar had given him a scroll of yellow paper tied up with a red ribbon.

It didn't look like a very good present to Atticus. You couldn't wear it or eat it or lie down on it. He wondered what it could be.

'It's your family tree, darling,' Mrs Cheddar said, beaming at her husband.

Atticus was puzzled. He'd heard of an oak tree and a horse chestnut tree and a Christmas tree, but not a *family* tree. Besides, it wasn't a tree. It was a bit of paper.

'It tells you about your ancestors,' Mrs Cheddar explained. 'You know, who your great-great-great-grandparents were.'

That would be interesting, thought Atticus. Atticus was an orphan. He didn't even know who his *parents* were, let alone his great-great-great-grandparents.

'I thought you'd like it,' said Mrs Cheddar to her husband, 'because you're so keen on family traditions, especially at Christmas.'

'I love it!' Inspector Cheddar gave her a kiss on the cheek. 'Come on, kids, let's see if we're descended from anyone famous.' He squeezed in between Callie and Michael on the sofa.

Atticus wanted to see too so he sat on Michael's lap.

Mrs Cheddar perched on the arm of the sofa.

Inspector Cheddar untied the ribbon and unrolled the piece of paper.

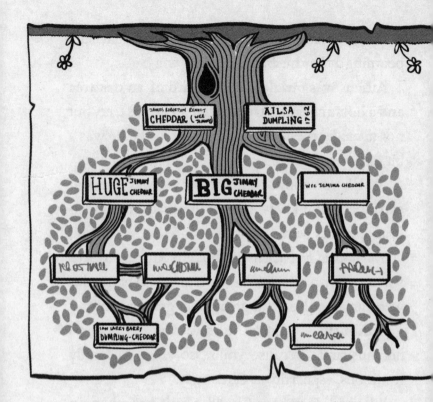

Atticus squinted at it. Now he could see why it was called a family tree. On the paper a chart had been drawn. It had lots of lines at the bottom that looked like branches and got narrower as it went up the page, like an upside-down tree. Beside each branch was the name of one of Inspector Cheddar's ancestors.

'The earliest trace of the Cheddar family is the

8

Scottish Cheddars of Biggnaherry,' Mrs Cheddar pointed to the name at the top of the chart.

'James Robertson Rennet Cheddar, also known as Wee Jimmy Cheddar,' Callie read.

Atticus listened, fascinated.

'He was a cheesemaker from the Isle of Mull,' said Mrs Cheddar. 'That's why he was given the name Cheddar. He married Ailsa Dumpling in 1762 and they settled near Biggnaherry, where she was from.'

Atticus watched her trace three lines with her finger under Wee Jimmy's name. 'Wee Jimmy and Ailsa had three children.' She waited for Callie to read the names.

'Huge Jimmy, Big Jimmy and Wee Jemima,' Callie said.

Atticus was getting the hang of it now. Underneath the names of Huge Jimmy, Big Jimmy and Wee Jemima were the names of *their* children and the people *they* married and so on and so on until the chart got down to Inspector Cheddar, whose full name, interestingly enough, was Ian Larry Barry Dumpling Cheddar.

'The Scottish Cheddars of Biggnaherry,' said

Inspector Cheddar. 'Well I never! I always wondered why one of my middle names was Dumpling.'

'I didn't know you were Scottish, Dad!' said Callie.

'Neither did I,' said Inspector Cheddar. 'You learn something every day.'

'Where's Big and Hairy?' Michael asked.

'It's not "big and hairy", Michael,' said Inspector Cheddar, affronted. 'It's Biggnaherry.'

'It's in the Highlands,' Mrs Cheddar told them, 'at the edge of a great moor. I looked it up on the map. We should go sometime, so Dad can learn more about his roots.'

Just then there was a loud roar from a motorbike outside, shortly followed by a knock at the front door. Mrs Cheddar went to open it. It was Mrs Tucker, the family's child minder. She took off her motorbike helmet and hung it on the coat stand.

'Merry Christmas!' she said, coming into the sitting room. 'I hope you don't have any plans for New Year.'

'No, not really,' Mrs Cheddar replied.

'Well, you do now,' Mrs Tucker said. 'Mr Tucker's cousin has invited us all for Hogmanay.'

'What's Hogmanay?' asked Callie.

'It's a Scottish New Year's Eve party,' said Mrs Tucker.

That sounded fun, thought Atticus. He liked parties. People dropped lots of food on the floor that he hoovered up without anyone noticing.

'Mr Tucker's cousin lives in the Highlands,' Mrs Tucker added.

'Whereabouts in the Highlands?' asked Michael.

'At Biggnaherry,' said Mrs Tucker. 'On the moor. Why?' she asked, seeing the expression on Inspector Cheddar's face. 'Do you know it?'

'Biggnaherry!' Inspector Cheddar gasped. 'That's where my ancestors are from. What a stroke of luck!' He showed Mrs Tucker his family tree. 'Is Mr Tucker's cousin called Dumpling, by any chance?' he said. 'We might be related.'

'No. He's called Don McMucker,' said Mrs Tucker. 'His wife's called Debs.'

'Hmmm . . .' Inspector Cheddar started searching about on the family tree for any trace of the McMuckers.

'We'd love to go, Mrs Tucker,' said Mrs Cheddar. 'Thank you.'

'Good,' said Mrs Tucker. 'I'll tell Herman to book the train tickets. Bones is coming too so Atticus will have some company.'

Atticus purred throatily. Bones was Mr Tucker's ship's cat. She and Atticus were very good friends and had been on several adventures together.

'Oh, and Aysha's asked if we can look after Mimi for a few days,' Mrs Tucker said, 'so she's coming as well.'

Atticus's purr deepened even more. Mimi, the pretty Burmese, was his best friend in the whole world.

'Now, how about some presents?' Mrs Tucker went to get her basket.

'Yes, please!' said the children, excited. Mrs Tucker was also an MI6 agent in her spare time, so she usually came up with some really good presents.

'These are for you, Michael, and this one's for Callie.' She handed them two parcels.

'Night-vision goggles!' exclaimed Michael. 'Thanks, Mrs Tucker! I've always wanted some of those.'

'You're welcome,' said Mrs Tucker.

Atticus regarded them with interest. He didn't need night-vision goggles because cats can see in the dark.

Callie's present was a wristwatch.

'It's not *just* a wristwatch,' Mrs Tucker explained as Callie put it on. 'It's got a secret camera in it and a microphone for when you're spying on someone.'

'Cool!' said Callie.

Mrs Cheddar unwrapped something that looked a lot like lipstick. 'Should I try it on?' she asked, removing the lid.

'Definitely not,' Mrs Tucker said, 'unless you want your head blown off. Twist the end, dear,' she said, 'only don't point it at anyone.'

Mrs Cheddar aimed the lipstick at the fireplace. BANG!

A small firework shot out of the end and exploded in the grate.

'Thank you, Mrs Tucker,' she said. 'I can see that being very useful.'

Inspector Cheddar got a big pair of woolly bedsocks. 'What do these do?' he said, fingering them suspiciously.

'They keep your feet warm,' said Mrs Tucker. 'Here you are, Atticus.' She placed a box in front of him tied with a red bow. Atticus pulled the bow open with his teeth and used his claws to prise the lid of the box off. He purred in delight. The box contained a large quantity of fresh sardines – his all-time favourite food – packed head to toe in ice.

'Herman caught them this morning,' said Mrs Tucker. 'He went out on the boat with Bones.'

'And we've got something for you,' Mrs Cheddar said. 'Be careful, though. It's delicate.'

Callie handed Mrs Tucker a parcel, which she unwrapped carefully. 'A gingerbread house!' she exclaimed. 'How lovely!'

'Michael and I made it,' Callie said proudly, 'with Atticus.'

Atticus regarded the gingerbread house critically. He'd got a bit sticky doing the icing, and the roof was a touch lopsided, but all in all it was a very good gingerbread house and he was glad Mrs Tucker was pleased with it. He thought Bones and Mr Tucker would like it too.

'Thank you very much indeed,' said Mrs Tucker. She turned to Mrs Cheddar. 'Now, about this trip to Scotland, there are a few things I need to tell you . . .'

'Why don't I make you a cup of tea, Mrs Tucker?' Mrs Cheddar offered. 'We can chat in the kitchen.

The children want to watch a film and I need to put the sardines in the fridge.'

'And I want to have a nap,' said Inspector Cheddar. 'All that cooking's worn me out.'

Atticus decided to get some fresh air. And there was someone he wanted to see. He slipped off the sofa, padded to the back door and hopped out through the catflap into the garden.

He felt excited as he walked down Blossom Crescent and turned right at the High Street towards the beach. He had never been to Scotland or celebrated Hogmanay before. And there was nothing much happening in Littleton-on-Sea. It was very quiet in the winter and since he'd called a truce with the magpies even *they* weren't causing any trouble.

He reached the seafront and strolled along the wall past the pier. The tide was in so he couldn't actually go and check the magpies' nest, but he could hear the three birds chattering away quietly to themselves. It would be safe to leave them for a few days, Atticus thought. They wouldn't risk

stealing anything shiny or they'd end up back in Her Majesty's Prison for Bad Birds.

He reached the beach huts. 'Mimi?' he called. He hoped she'd be there.

'Atticus!' Mimi meowed. 'Merry Christmas!'

'Merry Christmas!' Atticus gave her a kiss on the nose. 'I brought you a sardine,' he said, unwrapping one from his handkerchief.

'And I brought you a flower,' Mimi tucked it into the knot. 'It's from Aysha's shop.'

'I'm so glad you're coming to Scotland for Hogmanay,' said Atticus.

'Me too,' said Mimi. 'It'll be an adventure.'

'No, it won't,' Atticus said. 'We're just going for Hogmanay.'

'It's still an adventure if you haven't done it before,' Mimi insisted. 'Besides, it might turn into something else with you around!'

That was true, Atticus thought, as the two cats wandered back to Mimi's house to say hello to Aysha's baby. Adventures did have a habit of creeping up on him when he wasn't expecting them. And it had been a while since his last one: maybe it was time for another!

Meanwhile . . .

Under the pier, three black-and-white birds huddled together in a scruffy hollow made of twisted twigs. One was fat with ragged tail feathers, one was thin with a hooked foot, and the third – the leader of the magpie gang – was big and strong with glossy feathers and glittering eyes. His name was Jimmy Magpie.

'I didn't think the old place would need so much work,' the scrawny bird said sadly, surveying the ruins of their nest. It had suffered considerable damage in their absence and, although the magpies had been back for a while now, none of them could be bothered to repair it.

'It's not that bad, Slasher,' the fat one replied. 'It

just needs spring cleaning.' He poked a bit of twig back into place and removed a quantity of rubbish, which he threw over the side of the nest into the sea.

'Yeah, but it's not spring, is it, Thug?' Slasher argued. 'It's winter. It's bloomin' freezing and we've got nothing to keep us warm.'

'We could line it with seaweed,' Thug suggested.

'Too smelly,' Slasher said.

'What about some nice big knickers?' Thug's eyes gleamed. 'We could steal them off a washing line.'

'No one hangs up their washing in winter, stupid!' Slasher retorted. 'They put it in the tumble dryer.'

'What if they don't have a tumble dryer?' said Thug.

'Then they don't wash 'em.'

'Errrgghh,' Thug said. 'What we need is a furry nest snuggler.' He shook his head sorrowfully. 'I knew we should never have called a truce with Claw. He would have made a lovely nest snuggler. And we could have used his tail to make fluffy scarves.'

'Yeah,' Slasher grumbled. 'He'd've deserved it after everything he's done to us.'

Once, when Atticus was still a cat burglar, the

magpies had asked him to steal all the shiny things in Littleton-on-Sea from the humans for them. That was when Atticus met the Cheddars, decided to stop being a cat burglar, and threw the magpies in jail instead. Since breaking out of Her Majesty's Prison for Bad Birds the magpies had been on the run. It had been a great relief to them to finally return to their home under the pier when Atticus agreed not to arrest them after their latest crime spree, in exchange for their help and on the condition that they didn't try to steal anything else.

Jimmy put his head on one side and regarded Thug and Slasher coldly. 'Are you questioning my leadership?' he asked. It was he who had agreed the deal with Atticus. 'Cos if you are, I'll punch you in the crop.' He flexed a wing.

'No, Boss,' said Thug hastily.

'Never!' said Slasher.

Being punched in the crop by Jimmy was bad news on two levels. Firstly it hurt. Secondly it meant you couldn't talk for a while. And Thug and Slasher loved to chatter.

'Chaka-chaka-chaka-chaka-chaka!'

'Chaka-chaka-chaka-chaka-chaka!'

'Very wise, if I may say so,' said Jimmy. 'Anyway,' he continued, relaxing a little, 'we'll get even with Claw when the time comes. We need to make sure we're prepared. Then, when his guard's down, we'll whack him. *Then,* when we've whacked him, we can start stealing shiny things again.'

'Good plan, Boss,' Slasher agreed.

'So, with that in mind,' Jimmy grinned, 'I've got a little surprise for you.'

'Oh, Jimmy! A Christmas present!' Thug gasped. 'You shouldn't have!' He put his wings round Jimmy and gave him a big hug. 'Is it something shiny? Please say it is. Or one of them yummy chocolates in the foil wrappers? I love the gold ones.'

'Get away me, you big oaf!' Jimmy shrugged him off. 'It's not something shiny. And you should lay off the chocolate, Thug. You're too fat.'

'I am not!' said Thug, offended. 'It's feathers. They puff up in winter to keep me warm.'

'You're puffed up in summer too,' said Jimmy. 'It's fat.'

'What's the present, then, Boss?' Slasher asked. 'If it isn't something shiny.'

'An army training camp,' said Jimmy.

'What?' The two magpies looked at him in astonishment.

'An army training camp,' Jimmy repeated. 'To make us fit so that we can bash Claw and his do-gooding friend, Inspector Cheese, and steal all the shiny things we want without them interfering.'

'It sounds like awful hard work,' said Thug.

'That's the point,' Jimmy said.

'I dunno, Jimmy,' Slasher said, glancing at Thug. 'I'm not sure me bad foot's up to it. I've got Arthur-itis.'

'And I've got a bald tail,' said Thug. 'They don't take you in the army if your tail's bald.'

'Yes, they do, Thug,' snapped Jimmy. 'This is the Crow Brigade. They take anyone, even you. So stop making excuses, the pair of you. You're going whether you like it or not. Now take a look at this. It came with the pigeon post yesterday.' He leant over the nest and pulled out a piece of smudgy green card which was stuffed into an old screw hole in the rafter. It had black writing on it and a crow's-foot logo in the top right-hand corner.

RECRUITING NOW!
CROW BRIGADE
ARMY TRAINING
CAMP

Think you've got what it takes to be in the Crow Brigade? One week's basic training with our top commandos will sort out the tough turkeys from the dozy dodos amongst you.

Stamina, strength, hextermination and hexstreme survival techniques taught. Any member of the Corvus family may apply. Results guaranteed.

(Please note: fat, flabby and flightless birds are accepted. Also those with Arthur-itis. You'll either be dead or a fully functioning fighter by the time we've finished with you.)

'You sure we're members of the Corvus family?' asked Thug desperately. 'Only I wouldn't like to intrude on a family gathering, especially not at Christmas.'

'You know perfectly well we are, Thug,' Jimmy snapped. 'Crows, jays, jackdaws, rooks, ravens and *magpies* are all species of Corvus. And Corvids are the most intelligent birds on the planet. Except for you.' He gave Thug a peck and smiled to himself. 'What a lovely bunch of villains to spend New Year with!' he mused aloud. 'We'll have a whale of a time.' His eyes glittered. 'Well, I will anyway – watching you two suffer. Now go and pack. There's a kit list on the back.'

Thug suppressed a sob. 'Me poor old mum!' he said. 'What will become of her if I join the Crow Brigade?'

'What are you talking about, Thug?' asked Slasher. 'Your mum got run over by an ice-cream van four years ago in the High Street.'

'Oh yeah,' said Thug. 'Poor old me, then.' He set about assembling his kit from all the bits and pieces the magpies had collected in the nest over the years. 'What's a bungee rope?' he asked, reading from the card.

'Search me, mate,' said Slasher. 'I'm taking a bit of knicker elastic.'

'Good idea.' Thug poked about in the pile of stuff.

A little while later Jimmy Magpie went through the list.

'Black feather polish?'

'Yep,' Thug and Slasher replied.

'Stamps?'

'Yep.'

'Head torch?'

'Yep.'

'Swimming goggles?'

'I can't swim,' said Thug.

'Too bad. Take them anyway.'

Thug packed two bits of clear waterproof sticking plaster – one for each eye – with a weary sigh.

'Bungee rope?'

'Sort of.'

'That's it, then,' Jimmy said. 'We're ready.'

'By the way, Boss,' Slasher hoisted his pack on to his back. 'Where's the training camp being held?'

'Somewhere remote, that you can't escape

from,' Jimmy replied. He examined the flyer. 'It gives directions on here somewhere.' He found the information he was looking for. 'On the moor,' he read, 'near Biggnaherry, in the Highlands of Scotland.'

'That's miles away!' Thug protested.

'Which is why we'd better get going.' Jimmy took a last look around the nest. 'And remember, boys, when we get back – if you *do* get back, that is – Atticus Grammaticus Goody-Four-Paws Claw won't know what's hit him.'

'Chaka-chaka-chaka-chaka-chaka!'

Chattering excitedly, the three magpies flapped out of the nest and headed north.

'Hurry up!' Inspector Cheddar shouted. 'We're late.'

The next evening at Bigsworth station the Cheddar family were racing along the concourse with their suitcases. Mr Tucker had booked tickets on the sleeper train for them to collect on arrival, but the long queue at the ticket office meant that what should have been a nice relaxing journey had turned into something altogether more stressful.

Atticus slithered about in his cat basket. The cat basket was usually reserved for when Atticus refused to go and see his enemy the vet and had to be manhandled into the surgery by Inspector Cheddar. The reason he was in it tonight, Mrs Cheddar had explained, was because he had to stay hidden from view from someone called Great-Uncle Archie.

Atticus HATED the cat basket; he had no idea WHY he had to stay hidden from Great-Uncle Archie; and he didn't care WHO knew it. He had meowed the whole way there. He had also resolved to unpick the catch as soon as they got on the train and let himself out when Inspector and Mrs Cheddar weren't looking.

'Platform 17,' panted Inspector Cheddar.

'Here we are,' gasped Mrs Cheddar.

Their way was blocked by the train guard. 'Tickets, please,' said the guard. Atticus peeped through the grill of the cat basket. The guard was a large woman with short hair, big biceps and a moustache. A heavy set of keys dangled from her belt. She looked more like a prison guard than a train guard, Atticus thought. He stopped meowing.

Inspector Cheddar waved the tickets at her. 'We're in a bit of a hurry,' he said. 'If you don't mind . . .'

'I do mind.' The train guard stood in front of him. She took the tickets and examined them carefully. 'Have you got a ticket for the cat?' she asked, eyeballing Atticus.

'No,' Inspector Cheddar said.

'I can't let you board this train if you don't buy a ticket for the cat,' said the guard.

'But why do we need one?' Callie asked.

'The berth will need deep cleaning,' said the guard, 'for cat hairs. They get everywhere.' She picked one off Inspector Cheddar's sleeve. 'See?'

Atticus felt offended. He was very clean, thank you very much. Okay, he might shed a few hairs from time to time. But so did humans. That's why a lot of them were bald. And you didn't often see a bald cat, did you? (Except for the ones that were supposed to be.)

'We'd better get him a ticket, darling,' Mrs Cheddar said anxiously. 'We can't miss the train. The Tuckers are waiting for us.'

'Oh, all right,' said Inspector Cheddar, 'but I warn you, I intend to make an official complaint about this. How much is it?' He got out a five-pound note.

'Ninety pounds,' said the guard. 'One way.'

'*What?*' Inspector Cheddar exploded. 'That's more expensive than *our* tickets!'

'Do you want it or not?' The guard fingered her ticket machine.

Atticus glanced at the station clock. It was only two minutes until the train left.

'No,' said Inspector Cheddar. 'I'd rather walk.'

'You can't walk to Scotland, Dad,' Callie said.

'Callie's right, darling.' Mrs Cheddar got out her credit card.

The train guard handed over the ticket. 'Have a nice journey,' she said. 'We get to Biggnaherry at 5.21 tomorrow morning. I'll wake you up at 5.'

Atticus hissed at her. He had the feeling this was going to be a rotten journey.

'Atticus can share with you two.' Inspector Cheddar put the cat basket down on the floor in Michael and Callie's cabin. To Atticus's surprise he knelt down and opened the catch himself. 'Feel free to shed as much hair as you like,' he said to Atticus bitterly. 'We're paying for it.'

Atticus perked up a bit. It wasn't often Inspector Cheddar encouraged him to shed hair. Usually all Inspector Cheddar did was complain about Atticus getting it on his uniform. This was too good an opportunity to miss! Atticus exited the cat basket, jumped on to the bottom bunk, and began to groom his fur with long rasping licks, spitting the hair out as he went. He didn't want to get a fur ball.

'We're next door if you need us,' said Mrs Cheddar. 'The Tuckers are in the cabin beside that.' She glanced at her watch. 'It's bedtime,' she said.

'Can't we just go and say hello to Mr and Mrs Tucker?' Michael pleaded.

'All right,' Mrs Cheddar agreed. 'But you heard the train guard; we've got an early start tomorrow, so don't be long. And remember to keep Atticus hidden from Great-Uncle Archie.'

Atticus wished someone would explain a) who Great-Uncle Archie was, and b) what his problem was. 'Meow?' He stopped grooming himself and pawed at Callie's sleeve. Now that he wasn't in the cat basket any more, maybe they'd stop ignoring him.

Luckily, Callie got the hint. 'Great-Uncle Archie is Mr Tucker's great-uncle,' she told him. 'He was staying with the Tuckers for Christmas. He lives with Don and Debs normally. Mr and Mrs Tucker are taking him home to Biggnaherry.'

Now Atticus understood. Well, part of it anyway. He still had no idea why he had to hide. A thought occurred to him. Maybe it was because Mrs Tucker wanted to give Great-Uncle Archie a nice surprise when they got there.

'Sleep well!' The two grown-ups went through the inter-connecting door and closed it behind them.

'Come on.' Callie opened the cabin door and peered out. 'It's okay, the coast's clear.' She led the way along the corridor to Mr and Mrs Tucker's cabin. Michael followed her.

Atticus swayed to and fro behind them, the train wobbling and lurching beneath his feet.

CLACK-A-DE-CLACK! CLACK-A-DE-CLACK!

Callie knocked on the door.

'Come in,' said Mrs Tucker.

The children entered the cabin.

Mrs Tucker was in her Hells Angels nightie and biker boots. She was washing her face in the tiny sink by the window with Thumpers' Traditional GloBrite. Her sleeves were rolled up. Emblazoned on her forearm was a tattoo which read:

DON'T MESS WITH EDNA IF YOU WANT TO KEEP YOUR TEETH

'Kids!' she cried, drying her shiny face on a towel. 'And Atticus! Glad you made it!' She frowned. 'I hope you didn't have any trouble with that train guard. She tried to make Mr Tucker pay extra for his beard-jumper.'

Mr Tucker had a very bushy beard that was all mixed up with his woolly jumper. (Or a very woolly jumper that was all mixed up with his bushy beard.) Whichever way round it was, Atticus liked Mr Tucker's beard-jumper because very often it contained fishy morsels, which Mr Tucker allowed Atticus to pick out with his claws when Mrs Tucker wasn't looking.

'We did, actually,' said Callie. 'She made us buy Atticus a ticket.'

'It cost ninety pounds,' Michael added, 'one way.'

'Ninety pounds!' Mrs Tucker whistled. 'I'll bet your dad wasn't very pleased about that.'

'Not very,' said Michael.

'I'm glad she didn't see Bones and Mimi,' Mrs Tucker said darkly. 'I'd have pulled her moustache off if she'd asked me to pay ninety pounds each for them.'

'How come she *didn't* see them?' asked Callie. 'Weren't they in a pet carrier, like Atticus?'

Mimi and Bones were curled up fast asleep on Mr Tucker's pillow.

'No,' said Mrs Tucker. 'Luckily they were at the bottom of my basket, under the fish-paste sandwiches. I put them there to keep them away from Great-Uncle Archie. The cats,' she added, 'not the fish-paste sandwiches.'

So it wasn't just me who has to hide from Great-Uncle Archie, then, thought Atticus. *It was Bones and Mimi too.* He wished someone would tell him what was going on.

His tummy rumbled. Mrs Tucker's basket was tucked neatly under the bunk. Atticus sniffed at it to see if there were any sandwiches left. It seemed ages since teatime. He found a crust and chewed it.

'I still don't get why we have to hide the cats,' said Callie.

Atticus listened grumpily. Nor did he.

'Great-Uncle Archie doesn't like cats,' replied Mrs Tucker, 'especially black ones, like Bones.'

Didn't like cats? Atticus could hardly believe his ears. What was there not to like about cats? And what difference did it make what colour they were? Atticus knew what *he* didn't like. *He* didn't like the sound of Great-Uncle Archie.

'Great-Uncle Archie is very superstitious,' Mrs Tucker explained. 'He thinks cats bring bad luck, particularly black ones.'

'That's stupid,' said Callie emphatically, stroking Atticus between the ears.

Obviously! Atticus purred his agreement.

'I agree,' said Mrs Tucker. 'But that's what he thinks.'

'Where is he now?' Michael asked.

'Mr Tucker's taken him to the toilet. They'll be back any minute.'

Just then they heard a clunking noise. 'There they are now!' hissed Mrs Tucker. 'Don't let Great-Uncle Archie see Atticus or he'll have a funny turn.' She pushed the cabin door so that it was almost closed but not quite. The children looked through the gap. Atticus clambered up the ladder to the top bunk and did the same.

There was Mr Tucker. The clunking was coming from his wooden leg hitting the lino floor of the corridor. (His real one had been clipped off by a giant lobster during a voyage at sea.) He was pushing a wheelchair containing a very old man. The old man had a tartan blanket over his knees, a tartan shawl around his shoulders, a tartan hat on his head and tartan slippers on his feet.

'Here we aaarre, Great-Uncle Aaaarrrchie,' said Mr Tucker, bringing the wheelchair to a halt.

'Have you checked ma cabin for cats?' asked Great-Uncle Archie in a thin, reedy voice.

'Aye,' said Mr Tucker patiently.

'You sure there are none under ma bed?'

'Quite sure,' said Mr Tucker.

'What about in ma pyjamas?'

'No, none in there either,' Mr Tucker said.

Great-Uncle Archie nodded. 'I'll take to ma bunk, then. Where's ma stick?'

'I's got it somewhere!' Mr Tucker fumbled around behind the wheelchair. He handed Great-Uncle Archie an old wooden cane. The cane was topped off with a silver knob. Atticus peered at it curiously. The silver knob was in the shape of an animal. Engraved upon it were a snarling face, ferocious claws and a tail. The creature looked almost dragon-like, but it wasn't a dragon, Atticus could see that. He could also see that just beneath the silver knob two capital letters had been carved into the wooden cane in italics:

SD

Great-Uncle Archie grasped the knob and levered himself out of the wheelchair with the stick.

'See youze in the moorrrning!' Mr Tucker bid him goodnight.

'Ah hope so,' said Great-Uncle Archie, 'but ye never know.' His door closed with a bang.

Atticus heard the bolt slam.

Mr Tucker folded up the wheelchair and put it in the luggage rack at the end of the carriage. Then he stomped back up the corridor and entered the cabin. 'Give me strength!' he said to Mrs Tucker, as he removed his false teeth and put them in the sink to soak in some GloBrite.

'Cheer up, Herman, we've got visitors,' she replied.

'Atticus!' Mr Tucker's rosy face broke into a gummy smile. 'Kids!' He gave them a hug.

Atticus managed to hook a bit of fish out of Mr Tucker's beard-jumper. He gulped it down quickly before Mrs Tucker saw.

'Phew!' said Mr Tucker, sitting down heavily on the bunk and narrowly missing Bones and Mimi. 'I'll be glad to get Great-Uncle Aaarrrrchie home! This cat business is a right pain in the neck.'

'What are we going to do with the cats when we get to Biggnaherry,' asked Callie, 'if we can't let Great-Uncle Archie see them?

'Don't worry about that, 'said Mrs Tucker. 'I've explained the situation to Don and Debs. They said there's plenty of room in the cottage. Great-Uncle Archie won't know the cats are there. He spends most of the time shut up in his room watching TV. Now, off you go.' She shooed the children away to bed.

Atticus followed them back to their cabin. This time he barely noticed the *CLACK-A-DE-CLACK* of the train. Something was puzzling him. If Great-Uncle Archie disliked cats so much, then why did he have one engraved on the end of his walking stick? It wasn't even a normal sort of cat, like him or Mimi or Bones. It was a big, scary one, like a lion or a tiger.

And if Great-Uncle Archie's name was Archie McMucker, thought Atticus, *what did the initials SD stand for?*

At 5.21 a.m. precisely, the sleeper train drew into Biggnaherry station. The Tuckers, the Cheddars and Great-Uncle Archie were the only people to get off. Atticus, Mimi and Bones were the only cats. This time all three of them hid in Mrs Tucker's basket underneath the remains of the fish-paste sandwiches.

'Hide Atticus's pet carrier!' Mrs Cheddar hissed as she passed the luggage down to her husband. 'We can't let Great-Uncle Archie see it.'

'What a fuss!' Inspector Cheddar said crossly. 'If you ask me, all this cat business is a load of superstitious twaddle.'

Atticus was pleased that Inspector Cheddar actually agreed with him about something for a change, but otherwise he felt very squashed and grumpy. There wasn't much room in Mrs Tucker's basket; apart from the three cats and the fish-paste sandwiches, it also contained Mrs Tucker's Hells Angels nightie and Mr Tucker's spare false teeth. 'It's so annoying that Great-Uncle Archie doesn't like cats!' he complained.

'Tell me about it,' said Bones. 'I've been keeping out of his way for the last week and a half. He nearly had a heart attack when he first came to stay with the Tuckers and saw me in the kitchen.'

'Why is he so superstitious about cats anyway?' Atticus grumbled.

Mimi sighed. 'I hate to tell you this, Atticus, but I'm afraid it's quite common.'

Bones nodded gloomily. 'With black cats especially,' she said.

'But why?'

'Because in some places black cats are associated with evil spirits,' Mimi said.

'Evil spirits,' Atticus echoed. 'But people don't believe in that sort of thing now.'

'Some people do,' said Bones. 'Superstitions are like traditions. They last forever.'

'What happened when Great-Uncle Archie saw you?' Atticus asked her.

'He started ranting about something called the Cat Sith,' Bones replied.

'The Cat Sith?' Atticus repeated. 'What's that?'

'I don't know,' Bones said. 'Some sort of mythical cat creature, I suppose. He didn't say. But whatever it is, Great-Uncle Archie is petrified of it.'

The wind whistled through the gaps in the basket. Atticus peeped out of one of them. He could see the lights of the train as it pulled away. Apart from them, the station platform was deserted. He glimpsed a dilapidated wooden building with grubby paint peeling off it and boarded-up red doors. The platform sign swung to and fro in the icy wind. Somewhere a shutter or a window banged persistently. He shivered. The place gave him the creeps.

'There are Don and Debs!' said Mr Tucker. 'This way.' He wheeled Great-Uncle Archie down a ramp. The others followed with the luggage. Mrs Tucker picked up her basket. 'No meowing,' she whispered.

Car doors slammed. Atticus could see two pairs

of boots splashing through the puddles towards them.

'Welcome to Biggnaherry!' a deep voice said.

'Don!' cried Mr Tucker.

'It's a dreich morning you've brought with you!' an even deeper voice said.

'Debs!' cried Mrs Tucker.

Atticus felt a jolt as Mrs Tucker set the basket down. He removed Mr Tucker's false teeth from his tail, pushed the Hells Angels nightie cautiously aside with one paw and peered over the top of the basket. Two muddy jeeps were parked side by side in the car park facing the station platform. Don and Debs were loading Great-Uncle Archie into the first one. Atticus squinted at them. Curiously, even though they weren't related, Debs looked a lot like Mrs Tucker except she had long red hair, red biker boots, several nose piercings and a tattoo on her forearm that read:

DON'T MESS WITH DEBS IF YOU VALUE YOUR LIFE

Less curiously, because they *were* related, Don looked a lot like *Mr* Tucker, except that instead of a having a wooden leg and a beard-jumper attached to his chin, he was wearing a type of thick skirt with something very hairy attached to the front of *that*.

'It's a sporran.' Mimi's face appeared next to his. 'You wear it over the kilt. It's the traditional way to dress in the Highlands.'

More traditions, thought Atticus. He liked this one a lot better than the superstitious one about black cats being unlucky. Don's kilt was thick and colourful, like a big rug. It was just the sort of thing Atticus enjoyed lying on. And even from a distance he could see that Don's sporran contained some interesting morsels of food. He wondered if Don would mind if he picked them out.

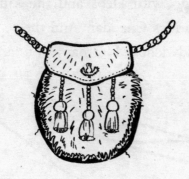

Don and Debs finished loading Great-Uncle Archie into one of the jeeps.

'Let's get you home!' Don closed the door on the old man.

Great-Uncle Archie wound down the window. 'Have you checked ma bed for cats?' he asked.

'Yes, Great-Uncle Archie!'

'And ma hot-water bottle?'

'Aye! Don't worry!'

'And ma electric blanket?'

'Yes, that too!' Don puffed out his cheeks. He glanced at Mrs Tucker. Mrs Tucker nodded meaningfully at the basket.

'They're in there,' she mouthed.

Atticus and Mimi ducked under the nightie. Atticus felt something nip his tail. It was Mr Tucker's false teeth again! He tried not to meow.

'We'll go with Debs and the kids,' said Mrs Tucker to Mrs Cheddar. 'And the ... er ... fish-paste sandwiches. Herman, you and Inspector

Cheddar help Don with Great-Uncle Archie.'

'Hooray!' Atticus heard Inspector Cheddar say in the kind of voice that meant completely the opposite.

He felt their basket being lifted into the boot of Debs's car.

'My tail's gone to sleep,' said Bones.

'And I can't breathe!' said Mimi.

'And my ears itch,' said Atticus. He pawed at the nightie. 'Let's get out.'

The three cats squeezed out of the basket. They hopped on to the back seat of the car and looked out of the window. Mrs Cheddar was putting the rest of the luggage into the boot with Callie and Michael; Mrs Tucker and Debs were comparing tattoos; Mr Tucker was admiring Don's sporran; Don was admiring Mr Tucker's beard-jumper, and Inspector Cheddar was making a note of the car number plates in his new notebook.

'I wish they'd hurry up,' said Mimi, shivering. 'This place is spooky.'

Beyond them, across the car park, lay the moor. It stretched away into the darkness as far as Atticus could see – bleak and desolate – rising and falling with the folds of the hills. Fog spread out in patches between the hummocks of heather, like ghostly blankets.

Privately Atticus agreed with Mimi – it *was* spooky – but he didn't want her or Bones to think he was a scaredy-cat. So instead he said, 'Maybe it's nicer in the daytime.'

'Maybe,' said Mimi. She pricked up her ears. 'What's that noise?'

Atticus listened closely. Somewhere in the distance he heard a faint rumble. 'Thunder?' he suggested.

'I don't think so.'

Atticus strained his ears. A low drumming sound was coming from somewhere on the moor. *THUD. THUD. THUD. THUD. THUD. THUD.*

The sound was getting louder. Whatever it was, it was approaching rapidly. Atticus felt his hackles rise. His instinct told him something was wrong.

'What was that?' Outside

the jeep Callie and Michael stopped what they were doing to listen.

'I'll take a look.' Michael grabbed his night-vision goggles from his pocket and walked off in the direction of the moor.

The three cats watched him anxiously.

THUD! THUD! THUD! THUD! THUD! THUD!

'I don't like this,' Atticus said.

'Me neither,' said Bones.

'Nor me,' Mimi agreed.

Atticus felt worried. Michael shouldn't be going on to the moor alone, especially not in the dark. He made a decision. 'You two stay here,' Atticus said. 'I'm going after Michael.' He leapt over the back seat and dropped down from the boot of the car on to the tarmac.

The car park was full of potholes. Atticus felt cold water splash his legs and tummy. Light drizzle fell on his back. Soon his fur was drenched.

Atticus gritted his teeth. He disliked getting wet, but it was too late now. And he wanted to catch up with Michael. He slipped along in the shadows keeping out of sight of Great-Uncle Archie. There wasn't much light anyway and his tabby stripes provided perfect camouflage against the gloomy backdrop of the moor.

THUD! THUD! THUD! THUD! THUD! THUD!

'What's going on?' Inspector Cheddar had heard the noise. He looked up from his notebook. 'Where's Michael?'

'Over here, Dad!' Michael had reached the edge

of the moor. He pulled on his night-vision goggles and adjusted the controls. 'I can see something! It's coming this way.'

Atticus hurried towards him.

Suddenly a deer broke cover from the fog. It crashed through the bushes at the edge of the moor and leapt into the car park. Michael jumped back, startled. Atticus dodged out of the way as the deer swerved past him and bounded through the car park past the jeeps and away into the darkness.

'Nothing to worry about, folks,' said Don. 'We get lots of deer around here.'

'Something must have given it a fright,' Mrs Cheddar remarked.

The back door of Don's jeep flew open. Great-Uncle Archie struggled out. He leant heavily with one arm on the car door for support. With the other he lifted the old wooden cane and pointed it shakily towards the moor.

'The Cat Sith!' he shouted. 'That's what it was runnin' from. It's out there on the moor!'

The Cat Sith? That was the thing Bones had said Great-Uncle Archie was so afraid of when he saw *her*.

Atticus swept his eyes over the moor. He blinked. Was he seeing things? A creature was creeping along between the tufts of heather. It was barely visible in the darkness; its fur was as black as night. But its shape was unmistakably that of an enormous cat.

'You're imagining it, Great-Uncle Archie,' Debs said. 'There's no such thing as the Cat Sith. Let me help you back in the car.'

Atticus strained his eyes. Was Debs right? Had he imagined it too? The creature had disappeared. He looked harder. No, there it was, slinking along through the dips and twists of the moor, moving towards Michael at a steady pace.

Michael! Suddenly Atticus realised what was happening. The creature was stalking Michael!

Atticus's instinct kicked in. He leapt forward, hissing and spitting. With his fur puffed up he looked twice his normal size.

The creature stopped in its tracks. It cast a malevolent look towards Atticus and curled its lip in a snarl. Then it turned around, slunk back across the moor and disappeared from sight.

Atticus felt Michael's hand on his back. 'Thanks, Atticus,' he whispered.

Atticus managed a purr. Michael was wearing night-vision goggles; he had seen the creature too.

'There's nothing out there!' The voice belonged to Inspector Cheddar. 'See?' The wide beam of a torch caught Atticus unawares. He screwed his eyes shut against the sudden glare.

'A cat!' Great-Uncle Archie cried. 'A cat!'

Atticus's tail drooped. *Oh no!* Now Great-Uncle Archie had seen *him*! He was going to get into trouble.

'I might have known!' Inspector Cheddar marched up. He pointed an accusing finger at Atticus. 'You were supposed to stay out of sight.'

'It's not Atticus's fault, Dad,' Michael protested. 'There was something on the moor. A big black cat; like a panther. I saw it. I promise you I did. It was chasing the deer. Atticus scared it off.'

'A panther!' Inspector Cheddar snorted. 'Sure! Next you'll be telling me there are tigers out there.'

'There are, actually,' Don had joined them. 'They're called Highland Tigers.'

'Highland Tigers?' Michael repeated. 'What are they?'

'They're wildcats,' said Don. 'They're very rare,

but they do exist.' He looked at Michael thoughtfully. 'Maybe that's what you saw?'

'Maybe,' said Michael. 'What do they look like?'

'A lot like Atticus, as a matter of fact,' said Don. 'Same size, similar markings, except without the white socks and the handkerchief, of course.'

Michael shook his head stubbornly. 'What I saw was black. And it was much bigger than Atticus.'

Don pursed his lips. He didn't seem to want to believe Michael for some reason. Atticus wondered why.

'A cat! A cat! A cat!'

Great-Uncle Archie was in full cry. Atticus couldn't help wishing he would shut up. It was proving to be a long night. He wanted to go to bed.

'What are we going to do now?' Inspector Cheddar asked Don crossly.

'We'll tell Great-Uncle Archie he saw a wildcat,' Don said. 'And that it ran away. Shhh!' He put his finger to his lips, picked Atticus up and tucked him into his sporran. Atticus tried not to sneeze. The hairs tickled his whiskers. 'It's all right, Great-Uncle Archie,' Don called. 'There's nothing to worry about. It was a Highland Tiger. It's gone now.'

They walked back to Debs's jeep. Don popped Atticus in the back next to Callie. He held the door open for Michael.

'Wait a minute.' Michael bent down and picked something up off the tarmac. It was Great-Uncle Archie's walking stick. 'He must have dropped it when he saw Atticus,' Michael said. The silver top gleamed in the weak lamplight. Atticus watched Michael trace the shape with his fingertips. '*That's* what I saw on the moor,' Michael told Don.

'Are you absolutely sure?'

There was something in the way Don asked the question that made Atticus's fur prickle.

'Yes, why?' replied Michael.

'Because that's a carving of the Cat Sith,' Don replied.

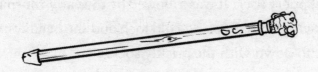

8

'Hup to! Hup to! Hup to!'

At Crow Brigade Army Training Camp, Thug and Slasher were having a horrible time. They were doing their early-morning workout. The first exercise was running on the spot.

'Knees up!' shouted the Sergeant Major.

'Why did I ever get talked into this?' Thug moaned. 'I'd rather get squashed by an ice-cream van like me poor old mum.'

'My Arthur-itis is killing me!' Slasher complained. 'I don't think I'll ever be able to hop again.'

The early-morning workout took place on the slippery rock. It was followed by the early-morning swim in the freezing-cold loch and the head-to-toe rub-down with the prickly sock.

'Keep up, you two!' shouted the Sergeant Major. About a hundred birds were taking part in the camp and they were all a lot fitter than Thug and Slasher. Most of them looked as if they came every year. Some of them even looked as though they were *enjoying* it.

'Star jumps!' shouted the Sergeant Major.

The two magpies heaved and puffed.

'Where's the boss?' Thug looked up and down the line of recruits.

'He's been moved to hofficer training camp,' said Slasher importantly.

'What's that?' Thug looked blank.

'It's where you go if you're smart, like Jimmy.'

'What d'you learn there?'

'How to boss other birds like us around,' Slasher told him.

Thug managed a chuckle. 'Jimmy'll be good at that!'

'Press-ups!' yelled the Sergeant Major.

Thug and Slasher dropped to their knees. They both tried one wobbly press-up and collapsed in a heap.

'You're pathetic,' the Sergeant Major said, marching towards them. 'We'll try bungee jumping instead. Where are your bungee ropes?'

The other birds produced long pieces of thick elasticated rope with hooks on the end. Thug and Slasher produced their knicker elastic.

The Sergeant Major stared at Thug in disgust.

'What's he looking at?' asked Thug.

'I don't think you were supposed to bring the knickers,' said Slasher, 'just the elastic.'

'Get up that tree!' shouted the Sergeant Major. He pointed to the tallest tree Thug and Slasher had ever seen. It was twice as high as their nest under the pier. Its branches were thin and sparse. They were covered with green lichen.

'I'm scared of heights,' said Thug.

The Sergeant Major flexed his wings. He was a big hooded crow – bigger than Jimmy. Way bigger, in fact. He put his head on one side and regarded Thug with intense dislike.

'I'm scared of heights, SIR!' he screeched.

'That makes two of us, then.' Thug gave him a pat on the back. 'And there's no need to call me sir – Thug will do.'

'I'm not calling you sir, you moron,' yelled the crow. 'That's what you're supposed to call me!'

'Yes, sir, sorry, sir!' said Thug.

'And I'm not afraid of heights.'

'I am,' said Thug.

'I know!' shouted the Sergeant Major. 'You just told me! And guess what? I don't give a flying fart if you are or not.'

'Language!' said Thug mildly.

The Sergeant Major grabbed him by the throat. 'Get up that tree, soldier, or I'll pull the rest of your tail feathers out one by one and make you eat them.'

'Better do what he says, Thug, me old mate,' said Slasher.

The two birds flapped unsteadily up to the top of the tree to join the others.

'Spread out in a line!' the Sergeant Major ordered.

The birds got into position. Thug and Slasher slipped and slithered on the lichen, banging into everyone else.

'Watch it!' yelled the Sergeant Major.

Eventually they found a space.

'Now hook your rope to the branch.'

The other birds slung their hooks over the branch.

'I don't have a hook!' said Slasher in panic. He examined his claws. 'Except my foot.'

'Use that then,' barked the Sergeant Major. 'Stay on the branch and anchor Birdbrain.'

'Who's Birdbrain?' asked Thug, looking round.

'You, you idiot! Now tie the other end of the rope to your ankles.'

The other birds did as they were instructed.

Thug allowed Slasher to loop the knicker elastic around his legs and tie it in a knot. 'I don't think this is a good idea,' he said.

'Don't worry, mate.' Slasher took hold of the other end of the knicker elastic in his wings. 'I've got you. And it's better than eating your own tail feathers.'

'Jump!' shouted the Sergeant Major.

'Goodbye, cruel world,' said Thug. He launched himself off the branch and pitched thirty metres head first into the heather.

'I thought you said you'd got me!'

Half an hour later, Thug was sitting up in the field hospital with a dirty bandage around his head. He'd been carted off the moor in a stretcher by two para-magpies.

'I told you my Arthur-itis was playing up,' Slasher apologised. 'I couldn't take the weight.'

'Are you saying I'm fat?' asked Thug.

'Not *fat*, exactly, just heavy,' Slasher said tactfully. Thug looked as if he was about to cry. 'Anyway, listen, I got some news to cheer you up, from Jimmy.'

'What news?'

Slasher leant towards him. 'It's a secret.'

'You not gonna tell me, then?' asked Thug in a peeved voice.

'I am gonna tell you, but you mustn't tell anyone else.'

'Okay,' Thug agreed.

'We're training for something BIG,' said Slasher.

'What?'

'I dunno. Jimmy heard it from the Wing Commander – the bird what's in charge of the brigade. He said it involves *treasure*.'

'Treasure!' Thug's eyes lit up. 'You mean glittery things?'

'Very glittery things, I believe, me old mate. Very glittery indeed. But no one's supposed to know except the hofficers cos all the birds in the Crow Brigade are 'orrible crooks and thieves.'

'Like us, you mean?' said Thug.

'Yeah, like us.' Slasher chuckled. 'And if they find out about it they might try to steal it for themselves.'

'Isn't that what we want to do?' asked Thug.

'Yeah,' said Slasher. 'It is. But we don't want *them* to know that.'

'Gotcha!' said Thug, his eyes full of cunning.

'Jimmy's gonna find out what it's all about. Then he's going to work out a plan. Meanwhile we've got to stick it out with Sergeant Major Bigmouth and not tell anyone what we know. Think you can manage that?'

Thug nodded. Where glittery things were involved even he could keep a secret.

'Good.' Slasher rose painfully to his feet. 'Now remember, don't breathe a word to any-birdy or it'll be Jimmy who pulls out your tail feathers and makes you eat them.'

Don and Debs' cottage lay about two miles outside the village of Biggnaherry, on a single-track road that wound its way across the moor.

It was getting light as the visitors finally arrived at the cottage.

'Wait here with the cats,' Debs told the kids. 'We'll put Great-Uncle Archie into bed and then get breakfast.'

That sounded like an excellent idea to Atticus. After breakfast he envisaged a nice lie-down until lunchtime and quite possibly another one after that until teatime.

As soon as the grown-ups had gone indoors Michael let himself out of the car.

'What are you doing?' said Callie.

'I want to look for that animal I saw at the station,' Michael replied. 'I found some binoculars in the car. Come on.'

Callie followed with Mimi, Bones and Atticus.

Michael swept the moor with the binoculars.

'You'll never find it out there,' Callie said, surveying the landscape.

The cottage was completely isolated; surrounded by the moor as far as the eye could see.

Atticus looked keenly at his surroundings. The moor was still bleak and desolate but it *did* look nicer in the day, a lot nicer in fact. He'd never imagined there could be so many different shades of brown and green, or that the combined effect of all of them could be so colourful. The moor had a rugged beauty that surprised him. Atticus felt suddenly alert. He raised his tail and

arched his back, allowing the icy blast to ruffle his fur.

'Are you *sure* you saw something?' Callie asked her brother.

'Quite sure,' said Michael. 'Atticus saw it too. Didn't you, Atticus?'

Atticus meowed. He *thought* he had, but now in the light of day he began to wonder if the darkness had played tricks on him. He sniffed. The Highland air smelled sharp and clean. It made the insides of his nostrils tingle. He lifted his head and took another breath. The wind rippled his ears and whiskers.

'Look at Atticus,' Callie said in delight. 'He seems really at home here!'

'It's the Highland Tiger in him,' Don's voice said. 'I think he must be related to our Scottish

wildcats somewhere along the line.' He crossed the road and stood beside them.

Atticus couldn't help feeling a teeny bit flattered. A tiger! Him! He wished someone could draw *his* family tree so that he could find out if what Don said was true. He took a few steps out on to the moor between some scrubby bushes. The grass felt springy between the pads of his paws.

'Come on,' he meowed to Bones and Mimi. 'Let's go and explore.'

'No thanks,' said Bones.

'Do you think we should?' asked Mimi.

Atticus felt a bit annoyed that they didn't want to join him. They weren't being very adventurous! He took a few more steps.

'See how well camouflaged he is?' Don observed.

'I can hardly see him!' said Callie.

'Don't let him go too far,' Don warned the children. 'The moor's a dangerous place, especially in winter. You need to

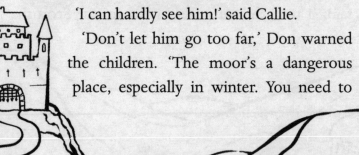

watch out for the birds of prey. And it's easy to get lost.'

Atticus hesitated. Of course he didn't want to get lost; or be attacked by a bird of prey; or the creature they had seen at the station, if it really did exist. But a part of him still wanted to explore the moor. It was so wild and beautiful. He almost wished he *was* a Highland Tiger.

'What's that place over there?' Callie asked. She pointed to a dark building on the horizon.

'That's Biggnaherry Castle,' said Don. 'All this land belongs to it. Debs and I work for the owner.'

'Doing what?' asked Michael.

'Looking after the place, mostly,' said Don. 'I do the cooking. Debs mends the roof. In the summer we teach people how to fish on the loch. In the winter it can be a bit gloomy because it gets dark so early; that's why the owner always holds a big party at Hogmanay and invites everyone from the village. It's a Biggnaherry tradition.

Another one! thought Atticus.

'Is that the party we're going to?' asked Michael.

Don nodded. 'If you behave yourselves!'

'I'd love to own a castle,' Callie sighed.

'Who does own it?' Michael wanted to know.

'Lady Jemima Dumpling,' said Don.

'No way!' Michael exclaimed.

Don looked at him questioningly.

'Dad's middle name is Dumpling!' Michael said. 'And his great-grandmother was called Jemima.' He told Don about the family tree. 'Do you think Dad and Lady Jemima might be related?'

'I hope for his sake he isn't,' said Don.

'What do you mean?' asked Callie.

There was silence for a moment. The children looked at Don expectantly.

'It's all to do with the Cat Sith,' Don said finally.

The Cat Sith! Atticus glanced at Mimi and Bones.

'Come on,' said Don. He strode back to the cottage. 'I'll tell you over breakfast.'

Everyone sat round the big oak table in the kitchen at the cottage, except Atticus, Bones and Mimi, who sat round the fire. Great-Uncle Archie had been put safely to bed with his hot-water bottle.

A mouth-watering smell came from the table. Debs and Mr Tucker had prepared smokies for breakfast. 'They're a bit like kippers,' Debs said, 'only more fishy. Don catches them in the loch and smokes them himself.'

'I's might try one in me pipe,' said Mr Tucker. He got his pipe out of his trousers and started stuffing fish into it.

'Not that kind of smokes, Herman,' said Mrs Tucker impatiently. 'Don means smoking them to eat.'

 Mr Tucker paid no attention. Debs put down three plates of food for the cats. Atticus tucked in greedily, licking the salty butter off his nose. Smokies were delicious. They were almost as yummy as sardines.

'You'll never guess what, Dad,' Callie said. 'Biggnaherry Castle is owned by someone called Lady Jemima Dumpling.'

'Lady Jemima DUMPLING!' Inspector Cheddar nearly swooned. 'We must be related! Lord Ian Larry Barry Dumpling Cheddar.' He rolled the name around his tongue. 'That's well posh.'

'Don't get too excited, Dad,' Michael said. 'Just because your middle name's Dumpling it doesn't make you a lord. And Don says it's not a good thing to be a Dumpling, anyway.'

'Why ever not?' asked Mrs Cheddar.

'Because of the Dumpling family curse,' said Don.

The Dumpling family curse! Atticus stopped slurping butter and drew closer to the table.

'It's to do with the Cat Sith,' said Michael.

'The Cat Sith? You mean that thing Great-Uncle

Archie was going on about at the station?' asked Inspector Cheddar, astonished.

Don nodded.

'Oh dear,' said Mrs Cheddar in a worried voice. 'Maybe we should go home before anything goes wrong.'

Atticus knew what she meant. Inspector Cheddar did have a bad habit of getting cursed every now and then. It was usually Atticus who had to save him.

'No way,' said Inspector Cheddar stubbornly. 'Us Dumplings stick together. And there's no such thing as the Cat Sith. Debs said so.'

Everyone looked at Debs.

'Well,' said Debs, 'I've never seen it personally, but plenty of people at Biggnaherry say they have, especially since the winter began. No one wants to go anywhere near the castle at the moment unless they have to.' She sighed. 'There's even talk in the village of cancelling the Hogmanay party, I'm afraid. Most of the volunteers have dropped out.'

'We can't let that happen!' said Mrs Tucker, seeing the kids' disappointed faces. 'Maybe I can help instead?' Mrs Cheddar was very good at organising things – it was part of her job.

'We'll ask her ladyship this afternoon,' agreed Debs. 'But I know she's very worried. It was she who suggested we cancel the party – just to be on the safe side.'

Inspector Cheddar puffed out his chest importantly. 'I don't mind offering Lady Jemima round-the-clock police protection just in case. Luckily for her I packed my police uniform.' He practised a few karate chops. 'Tell her not to worry. Nothing will get past me!'

Atticus rolled his eyes at Mimi. He'd heard that before!

'You'd better tell us about this curse, Don,' Mrs Tucker said, casting a sideways look at Inspector Cheddar.

Atticus glanced at her. Mrs Tucker's face wore her secret-agent expression. It was the kind of determined look that told you something important might happen and if it did you had to be ready for it. All three cats recognised it at once. They pricked up their ears.

'It all began,' said Don, 'in Roman times.'

Roman times? Atticus was surprised. Surely even Great-Uncle Archie wasn't that old.

'At that time the country of Scotland was called Caledonia,' Don said. 'It was a wild place, inhabited by fierce warriors called the Picts. They lived in clans deep on the moors and in the forests.' He paused. 'Their symbol was the Highland Tiger.'

Atticus felt a jolt of excitement. Mimi's paw crept into his. She liked stories too.

'Highland Tigers are ferocious creatures,' said Don. 'No one has ever tamed one. That's why the Picts adopted them as their mascot, to them the Highland Tiger represented freedom.'

Atticus felt a grudging respect for his ancestors. Being tame and belonging to someone else was all very well but it was true that the price of it was the freedom to do what you wanted.

'The rest of Britain was quickly conquered by the Romans,' continued Don, 'but not Caledonia. The Picts caused them such problems that the Romans built a wall to keep them at bay.'

'Hadrian's Wall!' Michael exclaimed. 'We've learned about that at school.'

Don nodded. 'But the Romans didn't give up on conquering Caledonia. They sent a legion of soldiers into the Highlands to defeat the Picts once and for all.' He paused. 'None of them ever returned.'

'What happened to them?' asked Mrs Cheddar.

'No one knows for sure,' said Don. 'Some say they perished in the cold winter, others that they were killed by the Picts.' He paused. 'But here at Biggnaherry, the local people believe it was the work of the Cat Sith.'

Inspector Cheddar snorted.

'Shhhh,' Mrs Tucker scolded him. 'Listen.'

Don resumed his story. 'The leader of the Picts at that time was a man called Domplagan – that's

 the Gaelic origin of the name Dumpling. Domplagan was the founder of the Dumpling clan.'

'Wait! I need to make a note of this!' Inspector Cheddar got out his notebook and started

scribbling. Don waited patiently until he caught up.

'When he heard of the Roman invasion, Domplagan summoned the wildcats for a council of war.'

'Cats can't talk to humans!' Inspector Cheddar scoffed.

'Yes, they can, Dad,' said Callie. 'We just don't understand them, that's all.'

Atticus purred. Children were clever, like cats.

Don smiled. 'Callie's right. We humans have lost the gift of listening to other creatures, but in those days the Picts and the animals did understand one another.

'Domplagan asked for help from the wildcats. He explained that if the Romans were successful, it wasn't just the humans who would suffer. The Romans would build roads and settlements; they would destroy the wildcats' habitat on the moor and hunt them down for their skins.'

Atticus's ears drooped. Why couldn't humans just leave animals alone?

'The wildcats distrusted the Picts, but eventually they agreed to help. They said they knew of one creature that could defeat the Roman soldiers . . .'

'The Cat Sith,' Michael guessed.

'Yes, the Cat Sith.'

'But what is it?' asked Mrs Cheddar.

'It's a cat of such stealth that you don't see it until it's too late,' said Don. 'Of such strength that it can pull off your head with one twist of its jaws, and of such hunger that it can devour an entire Roman legion in one night.'

That was a hungry cat, thought Atticus. He could only manage the contents of two foil sachets of cat food at one sitting and that was one more than Bones and Mimi.

'Domplagan withdrew his men to their fortress on the moor at Biggnaherry – where the castle now stands,' continued Don. 'They heard the tramping of the Roman soldiers as they set up camp on the moor and the clash of steel as they sharpened their swords in readiness for an attack on the fortress at first light.'

Atticus's fur was standing on end. Don's story was electrifying! He gripped Mimi's paw.

'When darkness fell the wildcats summoned the

76

Cat Sith. It stole through the camp in the dead of night and devoured the Roman soldiers as they slept. The ones who tried to swim to safety across the loch were drowned by the weight of their armour; the ones who sought refuge on the moor had their bones picked clean by eagles and wolves.'

Atticus was beginning to change his mind about being a wildcat. It sounded pretty rough out there on the moor. He wasn't sure he'd take to it.

'The next morning the Picts let themselves out of the fortress and made their way to what remained of the Roman camp. They found all the Roman soldiers dead. Apart from that there was no trace of the Cat Sith.' Don paused. 'They also found a trove of gold and a standard in the shape of a great golden eagle.' He took a gulp of tea. 'And that's when the trouble started.'

'Why?' asked Michael. 'What happened?'

'At the sight of the treasure Domplagan became greedy,' Don said. 'He claimed the gold for himself. Not long after that, he abandoned the wildcats as his mascot and took up the Roman eagle instead. He built a huge castle where the fortress had stood. It was Domplagan, not the Romans, who began to destroy the wildcats' habitat by building settlements. And it was he who told his warriors to hunt the wildcats down.'

'But why,' said Callie indignantly, 'when the wildcats had helped him?'

'Domplagan didn't need them any more,' Don said. 'And he wanted to wipe the wildcats out before they could summon the Cat Sith against *him*.'

That was really, really mean, thought Atticus. He was glad he wasn't a Dumpling. He wouldn't want to be related to someone greedy and horrid like that.

'He didn't succeed,' Don said. 'In the dead of winter the remaining wildcats got together and summoned the Cat Sith for a second time. Domplagan thought the fortifications at the castle made him safe, but no door or window or wall is thick or strong enough to stop the Cat Sith.'

Atticus squeezed Mimi's paw again. He had a feeling this bit was going to be really good.

'The Cat Sith travelled across the moor and rampaged through the castle,' Don went on. 'It killed Domplagan and his men. And when the Cat Sith had finished, the wildcats went to the castle and hid the treasure to stop any other member of the Dumpling clan being corrupted by it like Domplagan had been.'

'You mean the treasure's still there?' asked Michael.

'According to local legend, yes,' said Don. 'But no Dumpling has ever found it and most of them daren't look.'

'Why not?' asked Callie.

'Because the legend says the wildcats set the Cat Sith to safeguard the moor. If any Dumpling ever tried to find the treasure, so the story goes, he or she would die at its paws. That is the Dumpling family curse.'

'Did Great-Uncle Archie try to find the treasure?' Michael guessed aloud. 'Is that why he's afraid?'

Don nodded. 'He thinks he disturbed the Cat Sith.'

'But Great-Uncle Archie's still alive,' said Michael.

'He's not a Dumpling, though,' Callie pointed out. 'He's a McMucker.'

'It wasn't just Great-Uncle Archie who went in search of the treasure,' explained

Don. 'It was him and Lady Jemima's father, Lord Stewart Dumpling. The two of them were friends. Neither of them believed in the curse, or the Cat Sith, for that matter. They thought it was Domplagan who had defeated the Romans and taken the gold, and that it was Domplagan who hid it when he went off to fight another battle. Thirty years ago the two of them went treasure hunting together.' He lowered his voice to a whisper. 'Shortly after that, poor Stewie Dumpling drowned in the loch.'

'I bet it was just an accident,' Inspector Cheddar said. 'They do happen, you know.'

Especially to you! thought Atticus.

'I'm sure you're right,' Don agreed. 'But Great-Uncle Archie believes it was the work of the Cat Sith. He thinks *he's* partly responsible for Lord Stewart's death. That's why he gets so upset about cats, especially if they're black.'

'Do you think the two of them actually found the treasure?' asked Mrs Tucker.

'I don't know,' said Don. 'Great-Uncle Archie's never breathed a word about it since the death of Lord Stewart.' He finished his tea and held the mug out for a refill. 'The only thing I do know is that he won't let that walking stick out of his sight for a single minute.'

'The walking stick?' Michael echoed. 'The one with the carving of the Cat Sith?'

'It belonged to Lord Stewart,' Debs explained. 'He gave it to Great-Uncle Archie just before he drowned.'

SD – Stewart Dumpling! Of course, thought Atticus. He should have guessed that.

'But if Debs and Dad are right and there's no such thing as the Cat Sith,' said Michael slowly, 'what did Atticus and I see on the moor at the station?'

'That,' said Mrs Tucker, rolling up her sleeves, 'is exactly what I intend to find out. There's something fishy about these so-called Cat Sith sightings. And it isn't just the smell coming from Herman's pipe. I think someone's after that treasure. The same someone who's stirring up all these rumours about the Cat Sith, probably. And I intend to find out who.'

Atticus purred his agreement. In his experience, where treasure was involved, there were usually villains not far away.

'I think we should go and see Lady Jemima first,' said Inspector Cheddar, 'and tell her that we're on the case and that there's nothing to worry about. I can ask her some questions about my ancestors while we're there.'

'All right,' Mrs Tucker agreed.

'I told you,' Mimi whispered as the humans got ready to go out again.

'Told me what?' asked Atticus.

'That this trip would be an adventure,' she purred.

'Blast it!'

At Biggnaherry Castle, Lady Jemima Dumpling threw the last of a thick wodge of used scratch cards in the bin.

'I lost again, Peregrine!'

She was addressing a bright-eyed falcon with a cruel, hooked blue-and-yellow beak. The feathers on its head, wings and tail were a steely blue-grey. Its throat was white and its chest and legs were finely spotted all the way down to its long sharp talons.

It gave a rasping squeak in response, put its head on one side and stared at her balefully.

'Don't look at me like that, Peregrine,' said Lady Jemima. 'I know you disapprove of gambling, but I

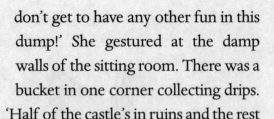

don't get to have any other fun in this dump!' She gestured at the damp walls of the sitting room. There was a bucket in one corner collecting drips. 'Half of the castle's in ruins and the rest of it's wet through. I'll have to ask Debs to get up on the ladder again later and check the roof.'

She went to the window and looked out across the moor. The sky was heavy with thick black clouds and the moor was shrouded in mist. Rain drummed persistently against the windowpane. 'It's raining AGAIN! I mean, can you remember the last time it *didn't* rain here, Peregrine? No? Well, neither can I,' she said bitterly. 'Although I can tell you as a matter of record that it was June the 27th, 1976.' She let out a deep sigh.

The falcon flew to a new perch on the faded brocade sofa and drew its talons along the arm. Stuffing burst from within.

'That's right, Peregrine, ruin the furniture, why don't you?' said Lady Jemima crossly.

The bird stopped mid-swipe. It regarded her coldly.

'Oh, I'm sorry, Peregrine,' said Lady Jemima,

throwing her arms wide in a dramatic gesture. 'It's just the weather gets me down. You know how I hate the rain.' She picked up a photograph frame from the desk and cradled it. It was a picture of Lady Jemima on holiday. She was standing beside a fruit machine with a big smile on her face holding two bulging bags of money. 'I do so miss Las Vegas,' she said. 'Such a nuisance I couldn't afford to go this year. I was sure I was going to win the EuroMillions in time.' She replaced the photo in its spot and approached the falcon cautiously. 'Will you forgive me, Peregrine?'

The falcon lifted its chin.

'Good boy.' Lady Jemima stroked the bird's throat with a long, painted fingernail. 'I didn't mean to be cross. Of course it doesn't matter about that silly sofa. Go ahead. Rip it up. Who cares anyway? When I've finished with this place you'll have a thousand sofas to sharpen your talons on. We just need to find that gold. Then, as the only heir to the Dumpling fortune, I get to spend it all!' She rubbed her hands in glee. Then her expression changed. 'If only I could work out that wretched riddle.'

Lady Jemima sat down on the sofa beside the falcon. She picked up a little black book from the coffee table and started leafing through it. She found the page she was looking for and stared at it for a few seconds.

One to lock, another to open,
Until then not a word be spoken,
Pretend to be what you want to be,
For that's when the Cat Sith holds the key.

It was a riddle she had read many times. Lady Jemima knew it off by heart. She recited it at bedtime. She sang it in the bath. She warbled it when she put on her wellies for a wet and windy walk. She mimed it when she massaged back into place the face filler the American plastic surgeon had pumped into her cheeks to get rid of her wrinkles on her last visit to Las Vegas. 'But what does it *mean*, Peregrine, that's what I want to know,' she said for the umpteenth time. 'It would be so much *easier* if we knew! Then we could simply find the treasure map that Daddy made all those years ago and . . . *BINGO*!' She let out a big sigh. 'It would save so much trouble.' She screwed up her face in concentration, muttering the words over and over to herself. After a few minutes she gave up.

'It's no good!' Lady Jemima snapped the book closed and threw it on to the coffee table in frustration. 'I'm never, ever, ever going to find that map. I've turned the whole place over a hundred times looking for it.' She scowled. 'That old fool Archie McMucker knows where it is. But I don't see how we can get *him* to spill the beans. He's completely barking. And I don't want Don and Debs to suspect anything.'

She took up a magazine instead and started flicking through the fashion pages. 'We'll just have to stick with our knockout Plan B, Peregrine. How are the preparations coming along, by the way?'

The falcon puffed out its chest and let out another screech.

'Good,' said Lady Jemima. 'I knew I could rely on you.' She gave his throat another stroke. 'I'm glad we're friends again. And we should look on the bright side.' She let out a peal of laughter.

'No one will come near the castle at the moment thanks to my lovely new pet . . .' She gave Peregrine a wink. 'You know who I'm talking about? So at least you and I won't have to endure that dreadful Hogmanay party again. Honestly, if I had to judge the hairiest sporran competition one more time, I think I'd scream!'

Something in the magazine caught Lady Jemima's eye. It was a fur coat. She showed Peregrine the picture. 'I'm desperate for a new one,' she said. Her face brightened. 'I think I'll make a shopping list for when we're rich.' She picked up a pen and paper and started writing:

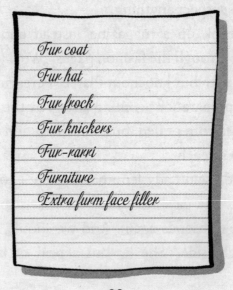

Fur coat
Fur hat
Fur frock
Fur knickers
Fur-rarri
Furniture
Extra furm face filler

Just then from outside came the noise of tyres on gravel. 'Who can that be?' Lady Jemima demanded irritably. 'I'm not expecting the McMuckers until teatime.' She went back to the window and peered out. Don and Debs' jeeps were both parked in the drive. Getting out of them were three cats, two children, a policeman, a man with a wooden leg and a hairy jumper (or was it a beard?), a woman with a basket and biker boots and another one with a clipboard. (And Don and Debs.)

'What on earth?' Lady Jemima hurried to the mirror to reapply her lipstick.

The doorbell rang.

'I'm coming!' She stomped down the stairs, re-arranged her angry features into a fabulous smile with a few upward strokes of the palms of her hands and threw open the door.

'Lady Jemima?' The policeman took his hat off and bowed.

'Yes.'

'I'm Inspector Ian Larry Barry *Dumpling* Cheddar.' He let the word sink in.

'Did you say Dumpling?' Lady Jemima blinked.

'Yes.' Inspector Cheddar beamed. 'Isn't it marvellous? I think we might be cousins two hundred times removed.' He whipped out the family tree and his new notebook to show her. 'By the way, Don's filled me in on the Dumpling family curse and there's no need to worry,' he added importantly. 'We think the recent sightings of the Cat Sith are a hoax but I'm here to give you round-the-clock police protection just in case. I brought my bedsocks if you want me to stay the night.'

Lady Jemima's mouth fell open. 'But . . .' she began.

'It's really no trouble,' Inspector Cheddar insisted.

'How kind,' Lady Jemima said in a strangled voice. She turned to Mrs Tucker. 'And you are . . . ?'

'Edna Tucker,' said Mrs Tucker. 'Also known as Agent Whelk. And this is my husband, Herman.'

Mr Tucker gave Lady Jemima a cheery wave.

Lady Jemima looked at him in astonishment. 'Why is he wearing his sporran on his chin?' she asked Mrs Tucker.

'It's a beard-jumper,' Mrs Tucker told her. 'His

beard got mixed up with his jumper when he was a baby. He's been growing it ever since, except when it got minced by some magpies, but that's another story.'

Lady Jemima digested this information. 'Did you say you were an *agent*?' she asked.

'Yes, I wouldn't normally tell you,' said Mrs Tucker in a whisper, 'as it's a secret, but I'm on holiday this week so it doesn't count. I'm planning to find out what this so-called Cat Sith creature is that people have reported seeing on the moor.'

Lady Jemima's smile slipped down her face. 'Oh,' she said. 'Jolly good!'

Mrs Cheddar stepped forward with the kids. 'And *we're* here to organise the Hogmanay party,' she said. 'So you don't need to cancel it after all. Don said something about the hairiest sporran competition. That sounds like loads of fun.'

'Yes, it's an absolute hoot!' Lady Jemima said sourly. Her smile was now upside down, like a clown's. 'What are *they* here for?' She glared at the cats.

'That's Mimi,' said Callie, 'and Bones.' She picked up Atticus. 'And this is Atticus.'

'He's not a *wildcat*, is he?' asked Lady Jemima, more brightly this time.

'No. He's the world's greatest cat detective. He's going to help Dad and Mrs Tucker with their investigation.'

Atticus and Lady Jemima stared at one another for a few seconds.

'Well, that's just dandy!' said Lady Jemima. She was developing a tic in her right eye. She pretended to cough. 'Blast it!' she said under her breath. She pushed the corners of her mouth back up with her fingers. Then, to her visitors she said, 'What a wonderful surprise! Why don't you come in and meet Peregrine? Don can make us some tea.'

'What was your great-great-great-great-great-great-great-great-grandfather's name?'

Atticus yawned. Inspector Cheddar had spent the last hour and a half questioning Lady Jemima about her family tree. At the insistence of Lady Jemima, Atticus had been placed in a wicker basket in the corner of the drawing room under the watchful eye of Peregrine, where Atticus had no choice but to listen to the pair of Dumplings droning on.

The basket had once belonged to Lady Jemima's dog (now dead). Atticus wondered gloomily if it had died of boredom, like he was about to. Even without Inspector Cheddar's endless questions, the atmosphere at Biggnaherry Castle was stultifying.

The tick-tock of the wall clock, the dark wooden furniture, the gloomy hiss of damp logs and the drip-drop of rain in the bucket were oppressive; not to mention the unblinking stare of Peregrine, who sat hunched on his perch, his eyes fixed on Atticus.

'Hilary Blair Deuteronomy Dumpling,' replied Lady Jemima.

Inspector Cheddar wrote the answer down laboriously in his new notebook.

'What was your great-great-great-great-great-great-great-great-GREAT-grandfather's name?'

'Brian Ryan Fingal Dingal Dumpling.'

Atticus wondered if Lady Jemima was making it up. He'd never heard of half the names she mentioned. But then again, he hadn't heard of many Scottish names.

'How do you spell that?' asked Inspector Cheddar.

'Which bit?' asked Lady Jemima.

'Brian.'

'It's Brian with an *i*,' said Lady Jemima, reapplying her lipstick, 'or it might be a *y*.'

Atticus glanced at the big wall clock. It was half past three. *I can't stand this any more*, he thought crossly. What he wanted to know was why *he* had been singled out for this particular form of torture. Mimi had been allowed to sit with Michael, Callie and Mrs Cheddar. They were poring over old copies of Biggnaherry Hogmanay party programmes beside the window where the light was better. And Bones had been shooed off down to the kitchen with Mr and Mrs Tucker to help Don prepare the tea.

He eyed Lady Jemima with suspicion. It couldn't have anything to do with the fact that he was the world's greatest cat detective, could it?

It hadn't escaped Atticus's attention that Lady Jemima Dumpling had not seemed very pleased to see them when they arrived on her front doorstep. Although it was completely understandable that she would rather have all her teeth pulled out than to have to talk about her ancestors for hours on end with Inspector Cheddar, you would have thought that she might be pleased to know that there was at least one other Dumpling in the world, even if it was Ian

Larry Barry. Yet at the mention that they might be related, Lady Jemima had reacted like a scalded cat. Nor had she seemed very keen to accept Mrs Cheddar's offer to help with the Hogmanay party. And at the news that Mrs Tucker planned to investigate the strange sightings of the Cat Sith on the moor with Atticus's help, Lady Jemima had practically choked. For some reason she had also seemed disappointed that Atticus wasn't a Highland Tiger.

Did she, he wondered, have something to hide?

He looked at her hard. Usually criminals had a shifty demeanour, but Lady Jemima's was not just shifty it was actually shift*ing*. Her face kept moving up and down. One minute she looked like a melted waxwork. The next she looked like a mannequin. It was all very odd.

Inspector Cheddar had prepared his next question. 'Who's your great-great-great-great-great-great-great-great-GREAT-GREAT-grandfather?'

Atticus threw back his head in despair. He'd rather help Debs mend the roof than put up with any more of his.

Luckily help was at hand.

'Sorry to interrupt, Dad,' said Callie, coming over, 'but we've put together a list of events for the party.'

'Hooray!' said Lady Jemima in the same voice Inspector Cheddar had used at the station to mean exactly the opposite. 'Let me see.'

Callie handed her a piece of paper. Lady Jemima read from the list. Her voice rose steadily towards a shriek.

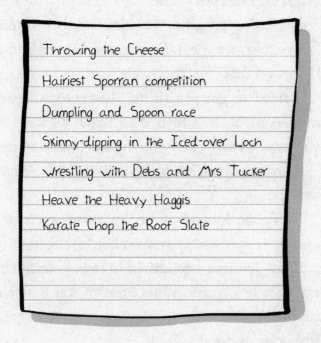

Throwing the Cheese

Hairiest Sporran competition

Dumpling and Spoon race

Skinny-dipping in the Iced-over Loch

Wrestling with Debs and Mrs Tucker

Heave the Heavy Haggis

Karate Chop the Roof Slate

'We put the last one in for you, Dad,' said Michael, 'as you're so good at karate.'

'How good?' demanded Lady Jemima.

'Yellow belt,' said Inspector Cheddar proudly, doing a few chops. He put his notebook on the table and grabbed the piece of paper out of Lady Jemima's hands. 'Throwing the cheese!' he crowed. 'I'll be ace at that too. Who's the reigning champion?'

'Debs,' said Mrs Cheddar, reading from the most recent programme. 'She won everything last year except the hairiest sporran competition. Don won that.'

'I need to get practising,' Inspector Cheddar said feverishly. He turned to Lady Jemima. 'Do you have a spare cheese in the kitchen I can use?'

'How am I supposed to know?' Lady Jemima shouted.

Everyone looked at her in surprise. A deep crinkly frown was etched on her forehead.

Lady Jemima smoothed it away frantically with her fingertips. 'What I meant was how am I supposed to ... er ... *throw* ... er ... against someone as good as you!'

'Ah,' said Inspector Cheddar. He gave her knee a friendly pat. 'I'll bet you're really good!' he said.

'Yes, well . . .' Lady Jemima brushed him off. She shot a look at Peregrine and jumped off the sofa. 'It's time to get rid of you.'

'Sorry?' said Inspector Cheddar.

'Ha ha! I mean it's time to get the . . . er . . . kids some . . . er . . . stew!' babbled Lady Jemima. 'They must be starving, poor things. I'll ask Don to see if we've got any in the fridge. Then you can all go home and eat it together and start practising for the party games. Come, Peregrine!'

She seems very keen for us to leave! thought Atticus. He wondered if anyone else had noticed. Unfortunately no one seemed to have. Even the kids were too taken up with the Hogmanay party plans to recognise that Lady Jemima Dumpling was behaving very strangely indeed. They followed her out of the drawing room.

'This way!' Lady Jemima led them down the stairs with Peregrine on her outstretched hand. 'Form a crocodile. Hurry up!'

Atticus was last to leave the room. He glanced around to see if he could see anything that would give a clue as to Lady Jemima's oddness.

The table was littered with teacups. (Lady Jemima's had an imprint of red around the rim from her lipstick.) Apart from that there was a glossy magazine, a shopping list of expensive furry things (and extra-furm face filler, whatever that was) and a small black leather notebook.

Inspector Cheddar must have left it behind! thought Atticus. He collected the notebook and knotted it carefully in his handkerchief to give to the Inspector later.

Callie popped her head around the door. 'Come on, Atticus,' she said. 'Lady Jemima is waiting for you!'

Atticus took one last look around the room. He would have liked to spend a bit more time there snooping about – in the desk drawer, for instance. It was bulging with papers. If Lady Jemima *did* have anything to hide, there might be a clue in there. And Atticus hadn't forgotten how to be a cat burglar – he could easily unpick that lock. He padded over to the desk.

'What is it?' asked Callie. 'What are you doing?'

Atticus hesitated. He didn't want Callie to think he'd started being a cat burglar again. She might tell Inspector Cheddar.

'Oh, I get it!' To Atticus's surprise, Callie giggled. 'It's a game! We can pretend to be real spies. I can use the secret spy camera in my wristwatch. Shhh!' She closed the door quietly.

It wasn't a game, but it didn't matter. At least he'd get to see the contents of the desk. Atticus reached out a claw. *CLICK!* The lock gave way.

Callie pulled the drawer open. She took out some papers and carefully photographed the pages with the spy camera. Atticus stole a glance at them. They looked much more boring than he'd hoped: lots of technical drawings, close-packed columns of numbers, and a folder entitled 'Proposed Redevelopment of Biggnaherry Castle' containing pages and pages of tiny writing.

'This is great practice for when I'm a spy!' said Callie, putting the papers back as they were. 'Thanks, Atticus.'

Atticus managed to mask his disappointment with a feeble purr. He clicked the lock back in place and jumped down from the chair. It was then that he saw the overflowing waste-paper bin. He removed one of the little pieces of card from it and popped it in the fold of his neckerchief with the notebook. Hopefully Mimi or Bones would know what it was. Then he followed Callie out of the room.

'Goodbye, goodbye, goodbye, good riddance!'

Lady Jemima watched impatiently as everyone got back in the jeeps.

'Are you sure you'll be all right?' asked Inspector Cheddar. 'I really don't mind staying.'

'Of course I will, you nosy beggar,' shouted Lady Jemima.

'Excuse me?'

'I mean, of course I will, you darling Cheddar,' Lady Jemima corrected herself.

'All right, then, but phone if you need me.' Inspector Cheddar lifted his foot on to the step of the jeep.

Peregrine gave a loud screech.

'What now, Peregrine?' asked Lady Jemima.

Peregrine flew to the ground. He opened his beak in a savage pose, hunched his wings, crept slowly along the gravel and nipped Inspector Cheddar on the heel.

'Ah yes,' said Lady Jemima, 'good thinking, Peregrine.' The falcon resumed its perch on her outstretched hand. 'Yoo hoo!' she called after Inspector Cheddar. He turned around. 'Can I borrow your bedsocks?' she asked.

'Pardon?' said Inspector Cheddar.

'I said can I borrow your bedsocks. I need them to . . . er . . . keep the draught out,' said Lady Jemima. 'The weather forecast is for severe draughts under the . . . er . . . duvet tonight.'

Atticus listened through the window of the other jeep. *Severe draughts under the duvet?* That didn't sound like something the weather forecaster would say. Why on earth couldn't Lady Jemima use her own bedsocks to keep out the draughts under her duvet? On the other paw, he thought, they might all be wet from soaking up the leaks from the roof.

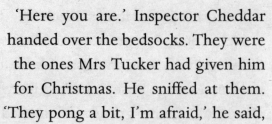

'Here you are.' Inspector Cheddar handed over the bedsocks. They were the ones Mrs Tucker had given him for Christmas. He sniffed at them. 'They pong a bit, I'm afraid,' he said, wrinkling his nose. 'I haven't got round to washing them yet and I do have a problem with sweaty feet.'

Yuk! thought Atticus.

'Perfect!' sang Lady Jemima.

Inspector Cheddar got into the jeep and the cars pulled away.

Lady Jemima waved the visitors off and hurried back into the castle.

'Well done, Peregrine,' she said. 'That idiot Ian Larry Barry gave me such a headache I almost forgot he claims to be a Dumpling. We need to make sure he never comes back here again. I'm not sharing that gold with anyone, except you, of course, and that's final.' She threw the bedsocks on the floor. 'You know what to do, Peregrine.'

The falcon fluttered elegantly down and collected one of them in his claws.

'Good boy.' Lady Jemima's face lit up in a malicious smile. 'Now go and give it to Chomper.'

At Crow Brigade Army Training Camp it was dinnertime. The recruits were sitting in groups around a campfire. The training exercise that afternoon had been called 'Eat or Starve'. The object was to dive-bomb and catch the small birds and rodents that lived on the moor and cook them for tea. But Thug and Slasher hadn't caught anything. That's why they were sitting down to boiled woodlouse while all the other members of the Crow Brigade were tucking into mouse kebabs.

'I don't know how they can live with themselves!' Thug said in disgust as he watched a jackdaw tear a chunk of meat off a wooden skewer and gulp it down. 'I mean, woodlice are okay – I don't mind eating them – but a cute little creature like that?

It's like eating your mum!' He shuddered. 'I'd rather eat my own poo.'

'Well, I wouldn't!' Slasher grumbled. He scooped up a beakful of woodlice and chewed on it. CRUNCH. CRUNCH. CRUNCH. He spat out the shells. 'Just cos *you* didn't want to catch a mouse didn't mean you had to belly-flop me every time I got close,' he said crossly.

'I wasn't belly-flopping you,' said Thug with dignity. 'I was practising my dive-bombing like what the Sergeant Major showed us and I just happened to land on your back. Besides,' he added grandly, 'I've got principles.'

'And I've got fleas,' Slasher opened one wing and flapped at Thug. A cloud of black specks hopped out of his wingpit and descended on Thug's head.

'That's not very hygienic,' said Thug, picking the fleas off and pinging them at the fire.

'Serves you right!' Slasher took another beakful of woodlice.

'Oi!' said Thug. 'Leave some for me!' He gave Slasher a push towards the fire. 'Mind my Arthur-itis!' Slasher squawked as he twisted over on his hooked foot.

It was Thug's turn to take a huge slurp of woodlice. 'Poo you,' he said rudely.

Slasher gripped him by the wings.

'Chaka-chaka-chaka-chaka-chaka-chaka!'

'Chaka-chaka-chaka-chaka-chaka-chaka!'

'FIGHT! FIGHT! FIGHT! FIGHT! FIGHT!' the other Corvids chorused.

'Pack it in!' The shadow of the Sergeant Major fell over them. 'I won't have insubordination in the ranks!'

'Insu-birdy what?' asked Thug.

'He means not doing what you're told,' Slasher explained.

'How about I throw you in the loch to cool off?' The Sergeant Major grabbed them both by the neck.

'But I can't swim!' Thug said.

'Good!' said the Sergeant Major. 'Then you'll drown.' He began to march them away.

'Leave them to me,' thundered a voice the magpies knew.

'Yes, sir.' The Sergeant Major dropped the magpies.

'Jimmy!' Thug and Slasher rejoiced.

'*Squadron Leader Magpie* to you.' Jimmy Magpie landed beside them.

Jimmy Magpie looked bigger than when Thug and Slasher had last seen him. His feathers were smooth and glossy and the luminous green-and-blue tinges to his tail and wings gleamed in the occasional moonlight. Thug and Slasher forgot their quarrel. They exchanged cunning grins. Life on the misty moor seemed to be suiting their boss. And that probably meant there were shiny things not far away.

The Sergeant Major was still watching.

'Come over here where I can beak you up,' Jimmy ordered. He led the way to a quiet spot out of earshot of the other birds. Thug and Slasher followed obediently.

'You not really gonna beak us up, are you, Jimmy?' asked Slasher.

'No.' Jimmy beckoned them close. 'I've got more news about the *treasure*.'

The three birds went into a huddle.

'It's like this . . .' Jimmy told Thug and Slasher the story about the Roman gold. When he came to the part about the Cat Sith, Thug shook his head. 'I dunno, Jimmy. I've already got a bald tail,' he said. 'I don't want my head ripped off as well. I won't be able to see where I'm going.'

'It's not real, you dodo,' said Jimmy. 'It's just a story the wildcats put about after Domplagan died to stop anyone else going after the treasure and spoiling the moor.'

'So how are we going to find the treasure?' asked Slasher.

'The wildcats are the only ones who know where it's hidden,' said Jimmy. 'The Crow Brigade's been hired to catnap one of them. Then the Wing Commander's going to hang it up by the tail and peck it till it tells.'

'Brilliant!' breathed Thug. 'I wish it was Atticus Claw he was going to peck,' he said a little sadly.

'Well, it isn't,' said Jimmy. 'Claw's tucked up in Littleton-on-Sea stuffing his face with Christmas pudding. And be warned – the wildcat may look like your average tabby but it will mince you. The Wing Commander says they're wild – real wild. That's why he needs the Crow Brigade. They're the only birds tough enough to do the job.' He prodded

Thug's gut. 'If I were you two I'd keep out of the way when the op starts and leave it to the pros. Only come out when they've got it tied up.'

'Do we all get a share of the treasure?' asked Slasher. He nodded towards the feasting birds and added boldly, 'Cos I've been thinking, Jimmy, if this lot found out we were trying to double-cross them, they'd slice us. Maybe we'd be better just taking our cut and going home.'

For once Jimmy didn't tell him off for being a coward. 'I wouldn't mind doing that,' he agreed. 'The problem is there is no cut. We're not going to get any gold.'

'How come?' asked Thug.

'Because the Wing Commander's working for a *human*.' Jimmy Magpie spat the word out. The magpies hated humans. It wasn't just Thug's mum who'd ended up under the wheels of an ice-cream van; over the years quite a lot of their friends had become roadkill too. 'And this human, she wants it all for herself.'

'Typical!' said Slasher. 'Greedy pig.'

'If she gets all the gold, what are we gonna get?' asked Thug.

'Bingo chips,' said Jimmy.

'What?' Thug spluttered. 'But they're not even shiny!'

'We might win,' said Slasher reasonably, 'in which case we'd get shiny coins. I quite like the occasional flutter,' he admitted.

'You won't win,' said Jimmy. 'The human will make sure of that.'

'How?'

'By having you all killed,' said Jimmy. 'She's got a pet panther called Chomper. You lot are its next meal. The only ones who get to go home when all of this is over are the officers.'

Thug began to sob. He got down on his knees and grabbed Jimmy by the ankles. 'Don't leave us, Jimmy!' he begged.

Jimmy kicked him off. 'I'm not going anywhere until I get my gold,' he said. 'Now give me a minute. I need to think.'

Thug and Slasher waited quietly.

Jimmy's eyes rested upon the other members of the Crow Brigade. Most of the birds had finished their meals. They were sitting around the campfire telling dirty jokes and picking their beaks. He pointed to the vagabond birds. 'Slasher, what was it you said just now about what would happen if we tried to double-cross them?' he asked.

'I said they'd slice us, Boss,' Slasher replied.

'Hmmm.' Jimmy nodded thoughtfully. His eyes glittered. 'That's given me an idea,' he said. He drew Thug and Slasher back into the shadows. 'Now listen closely, boys,' he whispered, 'this is what we have to do. Chaka-chaka-chaka-chaka-chaka . . .' Very quietly he began to chatter the plan to his gang.

14

At Don and Debs' cottage everyone was preparing for an early night, except for Inspector Cheddar who was still outside practising throwing cheese in readiness for the Hogmanay party. Atticus hadn't had a chance to give the Inspector his notebook yet. He'd been so tired what with the early start at the train station and the trip to Biggnaherry Castle that he'd fallen asleep in front of the fire as soon as they got back to the cottage, with the notebook still tucked into his handkerchief.

'Goodnight, everyone,' the children called.

'Goodnight.'

Atticus followed Mimi, Callie and Michael up the stairs to their bedroom, the notebook banging against his chest. They crept silently past Great-Uncle Archie's door. They hadn't seen the old man all day. Debs said he'd been catching up with his soap operas.

Their room was in the eaves. It contained narrow twin beds for the children. At the foot of each bed lay two soft blankets for the cats. Callie and Michael brushed their teeth at the sink and got into bed.

'I can't wait for the Hogmanay party,' said Callie sleepily.

'Me neither,' said Michael.

'Do you think everyone from the village will come?'

'I think so. Mum said she would organise buses so that no one had to cross the moor on their own. Then they won't have to be scared of the Cat Sith.'

'I wonder if that creature's still out there.' Callie shivered.

'I expect so,' Michael said. 'But don't worry. Mrs Tucker said it can't hurt us as long as we stay with the grown-ups.'

They fell asleep. Atticus removed the notebook from his handkerchief. The card he had retrieved from the bin in Lady Jemima's study fell out of it.

'Mimi,' he said, 'do you know what this is?'

Mimi looked at it carefully. Printed on the card were seven small silver metallic squares set out in a line. Three of them had been scratched off revealing different numbers beneath. At the top of the card were the words 'You Bet!'; at the bottom, 'Win £10,000! Instantly'; and on the back, 'You must be over 18 to play'. There was also a long telephone number.

'It's a scratch card,' she said. 'You pick three squares. If the numbers under the silver coating match, then you win £10,000.'

'That sounds good,' said Atticus.

'No, it's not good,' Mimi replied seriously. 'It's gambling. You have to pay to buy the card and the chances of you winning are virtually none so you actually lose money. Where did you get this anyway?'

'I found it in the bin under Lady Jemima's desk,' Atticus replied. 'There were lots of them.'

'How many is lots?'

Atticus shook his head. 'I don't know. I didn't have time to count them. But it was overflowing. There must have been hundreds in there.'

'Sounds like Lady Jemima's got a gambling problem,' said Mimi.

'You mean she can't stop?' asked Atticus.

Mimi shrugged. 'Lots of people get addicted. Then they lose all their money. Maybe that's why Biggnaherry Castle is in such a mess. She's broke.'

Atticus thought about this for a minute. 'Did you notice anything odd about Lady Jemima today?' he asked eventually. 'Apart from wanting to borrow Inspector Cheddar's sweaty bedsocks?'

'She didn't seem very pleased to see us,' Mimi said. 'And her face kept slipping.'

'I noticed that too,' said Atticus. 'I didn't really understand why,' he admitted.

'I think she's had plastic surgery,' Mimi told him.

She saw Atticus's puzzled look. 'Some humans have filler injected in their faces so they don't look wrinkly,' she said. 'The problem is, it needs topping up or it starts to sag, like Lady Jemima's.'

'Oh,' said Atticus, feeling thankful he was a cat. His thoughts returned to the strange occurrences of the afternoon. 'Was it just me, Mimi, or did *you* hear how Lady Jemima kept saying funny things and then correcting herself . . .'

Mimi nodded. 'Yes, I did, now you come to mention it,' she said.

'I'm sure at one point she said it was time to get rid of us.' Atticus scratched his chin.

'What are you getting at?' asked Mimi.

'It was as if she was trying to hide something,' said Atticus.

'Like what?'

Atticus's chewed ear drooped. That was the problem; he didn't know. He'd been hoping Mimi would be able to supply the answer. He decided to try another approach. 'Suppose Lady Jemima *is* broke,' he said, thinking aloud, 'wouldn't the obvious thing be to go after the Roman gold?'

'I guess so,' said Mimi, 'but what about the Dumpling family curse?'

'Maybe she doesn't believe in it? I mean, her dad didn't, did he?'

'But she *does* believe in it,' said Mimi. 'Debs said it was Lady Jemima's idea to cancel the Hogmanay party. She said Lady Jemima was worried about the sightings of the Cat Sith.'

'Then why didn't she want Inspector Cheddar to give her round-the-clock police protection?' argued Atticus. It was good to bounce ideas off Mimi. He felt like a detective in a film. Normally when he was out police-catting, Inspector Cheddar didn't pay any attention to what he had to say, partly because he didn't think Atticus was a very good detective and partly because he didn't understand Cat. With Mimi it was different. She was a lot more intelligent than Inspector Cheddar and she listened and came up with good ideas. He thought they made a great team.

'You think she's just *pretending* to be scared?' Mimi said.

Atticus nodded. 'Could be,' he said.

119

'But why?'

'So that no one suspects she's after the treasure.' A thought struck him. 'What if Lady Jemima wants all the money for herself?' he said. 'I mean, she looked like she'd stood on a cactus when Inspector Cheddar said he was a Dumpling . . .'

'That's true,' said Mimi thoughtfully.

'Which is proof that she doesn't want to share it. And she's got expensive tastes. She wants to buy a Fur-rari and redevelop the castle – and buy extra-furm face filler.' Atticus told Mimi about the shopping list and the documents in the desk.

'Redevelop it!' Mimi exclaimed. 'Into what?'

'I don't know,' Atticus admitted.

'We'd better have a look at those photographs Callie took,' Mimi said.

Atticus collected the wristwatch spy camera from where Callie had left it by the bed, pressed the switch on it, then clicked through the pictures until he reached the title page of the folder.

'Zoom in,' advised Mimi when she saw the pages of tiny writing that followed. 'Aysha says you should always read the small print.'

Atticus zoomed in. The letters became legible.

PROPOSED REDEVELOPMENT OF
BIGGNAHERRY CASTLE

Lose all your money in style without getting soaked with rain!

Biggnaherry moor to be dug up and replaced with a world-class bingo resort!

Attractions to include

For the grown-ups:

4 high-rise Las Vegas-style hotels with 1000 rooms each, equipped with the latest online bingo facilities and 'keep fit' fruit machines!

10 casinos open 24 hours!

2 shopping malls with scratch cards available at every checkout!

1 medical centre performing plastic surgery while you play!

For the kids:

Indoor waterpark

Junior bingo

Big cat zoo experience

Biggnaherry museum of traditional pastimes

Exhibition of stuffed wildcats

So that was it! Atticus felt sick with disgust. Lady Jemima Dumpling was planning to do exactly what the legend of Biggnaherry said the wildcats had been trying to prevent for the last two thousand years: find the gold, destroy their habitat and drive them off the moor. *And* she wanted to do away with all the local Biggnaherry traditions like cheese throwing and the hairiest sporran competition. They had to stop her. But how?

Mimi seemed more interested in something else on the list. 'She likes big cats,' she said.

'So what?' said Atticus. The big cat zoo experience seemed to him the most acceptable part of the redevelopment plan.

'Michael said what you saw on the moor looked like a panther.' Mimi's golden eyes regarded him steadily.

All of a sudden Atticus realised what she meant. Everything fitted. 'Oh, Mimi, you are clever,' he

said. 'The panther belongs to Lady Jemima, doesn't it? She's trained it to frighten people away from the moor by pretending it's the Cat Sith! So that she can go after the treasure without anyone knowing and use the money to redevelop the moor into a bingo park!'

'Precisely,' said Mimi.

'That's why she was so cross when Mrs Cheddar offered to help organise the party,' Atticus said. 'She didn't want the party to go ahead in the first place!'

Mimi giggled. 'She's not going to be very pleased when she finds out Mrs Cheddar's putting buses on from Biggnaherry,' she said mischievously.

Atticus turned off Callie's spy camera to save the battery. 'First thing tomorrow we'll show everyone the redevelopment plans,' he said. 'Mrs Tucker will know what to do.'

Mimi settled down on her blanket.

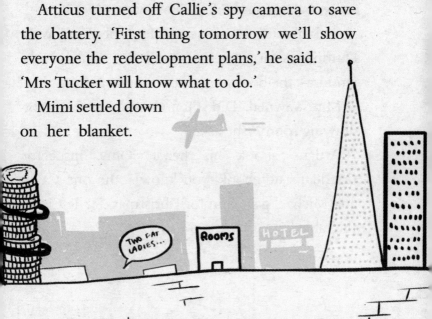

'Don and Debs will be really upset about all this,' she commented. 'They love the moor. It's their home.'

'I know how they feel,' Atticus murmured, thinking about the beautiful landscape and the fresh zingy air.

'You really like it here, don't you?' Mimi said.

'Yes,' said Atticus. Mimi waited for him to go on, but he didn't say anything else. He couldn't really explain how he felt about the moor or why he liked it so much or why it was so important to him to stop Lady Jemima from ruining it. He didn't really understand it himself.

Mimi groomed her whiskers carefully. 'What about Inspector Cheddar?' she said, changing the subject. 'Do you think he'll believe us?'

'I doubt it,' Atticus said. 'He's besotted with Dumplings at the moment. He thinks Lady Jemima's the best thing since tinned cat food.'

Mimi yawned. 'Did you find anything else in the drawing room?' she asked.

Atticus shook his head. 'Only Inspector Cheddar's notebook; you know – the one Callie and Michael gave him for Christmas. He left it on the table.'

'No, he didn't,' Mimi said. 'He had it in the jeep. He was making notes. You were in the other car with Debs but I definitely saw him with it.'

'Well, what's this, then?' Atticus removed the small black book from his handkerchief.

'It's a diary,' said Mimi, inspecting it carefully. She ran her paw along the spine. 'Look at this.'

Two letters were initialled on the spine of the book:

$$SD$$

'Stewart Dumpling,' breathed Atticus. 'It's *his* diary.'

The two cats exchanged looks. They were both thinking the same thing. Maybe the diary could lead them to the treasure before Lady Jemima found it.

'It can't be that simple,' Mimi said eventually, 'or Lady Jemima would have got her hands on the gold by now. I mean, she must have read this.'

'Well, then maybe it contains some *clues* which might help us.' Atticus was yawning too. 'Let's show it to Callie and Michael in the morning with the rest of the evidence.'

'Okay.'

Atticus closed his eyes. He could still hear Inspector Cheddar outside in the garden, grunting. Cheese throwing sounded like really hard work.

'Don't be long, darling.' Mrs Cheddar's voice floated through the window.

'I won't,' Inspector Cheddar promised.

'We're all going to bed now. Will you lock up?'

'Yes, I'll just try a couple more throws. I'm beginning to get the hang of it.'

The sound of more grunting was followed by the dull thud of cheese hitting the ground. 'One metre fifty-five centimetres,' Inspector Cheddar announced to no one in particular.

'He'll never beat Debs,' Mimi murmured.

'Or Mrs Tucker,' Atticus agreed sleepily.

The two cats began to doze.

'GRRRRRRRRR . . .'

'Did you hear that?' Atticus was wide awake at once.

'Yes.' Mimi jumped up on the window ledge. 'It's coming from the moor.'

Atticus leapt up beside her. The window was slightly ajar, to let fresh air into the room. It looked out on the back of the house, away from the road. Light from the kitchen window illuminated part of the garden.

'Inspector Cheddar's still out there!' said Mimi.

The cats watched as the Inspector hefted a big round Cheddar cheese to beneath his chin with his right arm, crouched down, whipped round in a circle and thrust it forward as far as he could. The cheese sailed into the darkness.

'He's got better!' Mimi said. 'He's thrown it right out on to the moor!'

Inspector Cheddar got out his torch. 'Not bad,' he said.

'GRRRRRRRRR . . .'

The growling was coming from the direction of the cheese.

Atticus groaned. Inspector Cheddar was useless at everything else. Why did he have to turn out to be good at throwing cheese? It was just Atticus's luck. Now he'd have to go and rescue him again, and from a panther this time!

Inspector Cheddar didn't seem to have heard the growling. He paced out the distance of his throw. 'One, two, three, four, five . . .'

'GGRRRRRRRRR . . .'

Atticus had the same feeling he'd had at the station: his hackles rose. The panther was definitely out there.

'Can you see anything?' hissed Mimi.

Atticus scanned the moor. The weather was frosty and the mist thicker than ever. 'No,' he said. He remembered the way the panther had stalked Michael. Its coat was so dark it was almost impossible to see it until it was too late – like the Cat Sith. 'But that doesn't mean anything. I'm going to have a closer look.'

'Be careful,' said Mimi. 'I'll get Bones to wake up the Tuckers.'

The back of the house was covered by a thick creeper. Atticus lowered himself on to it and wriggled downwards through the branches. He landed on the soft earth of the flowerbed and crawled forwards.

'Nine, ten, eleven, twelve . . .' Inspector Cheddar was still pacing his way slowly in the direction of the moor, scanning the ground with the torch. 'Thirteen, fourteen, fifteen, sixteen . . . ha ha! There it is!' Inspector Cheddar finally located the

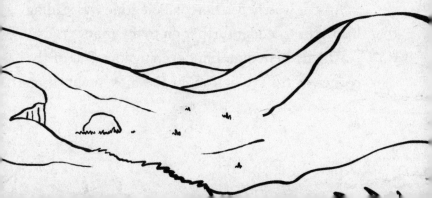

cheese. 'I wouldn't be surprised if it wasn't a world-record throw!' He bent down to pick it up.

'GRRRRRRRRRRRRRR . . .'

This time Inspector Cheddar did hear the noise. 'What was that?' He shone the torch around the edge of the moor.

Suddenly a huge bird plummeted from the sky. Atticus caught a glimpse of its blue-grey head and cruel, hooked blue-and-yellow beak before it pulled itself up in front of Inspector Cheddar and beat its white spotted wings at his face.

Peregrine!

'Crumbs!' Inspector Cheddar stepped backwards, startled.

The bird let out a rasping screech and snatched the torch from Inspector Cheddar's grasp.

'Give that back!' said Inspector Cheddar. He stumbled after the bird.

Atticus watched in horror. Peregrine was leading Inspector Cheddar further on to the moor.

Atticus went after him, keeping low. Out of the corner of his eye he caught the movement of an animal in the dense scrub. It was crawling forward on its belly, like him. *The panther!* It had something in its mouth. Atticus strained his eyes. The object drooped from either side of the creature's jaws, like a dead fish. But it wasn't a dead fish. Atticus could see that now. It was Inspector Cheddar's bedsock! So that's why Lady Jemima had wanted it: so the panther would recognise Inspector Cheddar's scent and chase him over the moor.

Inspector Cheddar was still running towards the torch.

'Aaarrrrrgggggghhhhhh!' Inspector Cheddar caught his foot in a divot and pitched head first into the heather. He sat up, dazed.

'GRRRRRRRRR . . .' The panther dropped the sock. It circled the Inspector.

'Go away! Shoo!' Inspector Cheddar had seen the creature now. He tried to crawl away. The panther's circles became smaller. It was closing in for the kill.

'Help!' Inspector Cheddar yelped, but his voice was weak with fear. His cries wouldn't carry to the cottage. Atticus glanced back, hoping that someone would come anyway. There were lights on in two of the bedrooms; Atticus could see the grown-ups moving around. But they wouldn't arrive in time. There was only one thing for it. He puffed himself up and sprang forwards into the circle beside Inspector Cheddar.

'Atticus!' Inspector Cheddar said. 'About time!' He pointed at the panther with a shaking finger. 'Arrest that cat!'

Somehow, at that particular moment, walking up to the panther and asking it to accompany him to the local police station didn't seem to Atticus to be a very sensible idea. Instead Atticus flattened his ears and bared his teeth. He hissed and he spat. But this time the creature didn't blink. It came on, Peregrine screeching encouragement from somewhere above.

'GRRRRRRRR . . .'

Then a different noise carried towards them on the wind.

'Sheeeeeeeeeeee!' Atticus's ears pricked up.

'Sheeeeeeeeeeee!' It came again.

'Sheeeeeeeeeeee!' And again.

The panther stopped circling. Its eyes shifted from its prey. It stared hard

at a point out on the moor to where a ridge of rocks stood. Very slowly, it began to back away. Then, in an instant, both it and Peregrine were gone.

'Thank you, Atticus!' Inspector Cheddar threw his arms around him. 'You saved my life!'

Atticus wriggled out of his grasp. It was nice being thanked by Inspector Cheddar for once, but it wasn't he who had saved his life. It was the other creature on the moor; the one by the rocks, the one that even Peregrine and the panther were afraid of.

A strong gust of wind ripped the mist into damp threads. Just for a moment, in the weak moonlight, Atticus had a clear view of the moor. Staring back at him from the rock was a female cat that looked very much like him. She was the same size and had beautiful markings and a sleek handsome face. Atticus knew he was looking at a Highland Tiger. He kept very still, unsure what he should do. Don had said the Tigers were wild – really wild; no human could tame them. Yet the wildcat had come to Inspector Cheddar's aid. Or was it to *his* aid, he wondered. Maybe it had nothing to do with

Inspector Cheddar; the wildcat was curious about *him*. It was looking him over carefully, taking in every inch from his chewed ear and red neckerchief to his four white paws. Atticus took a step forward. He felt strangely drawn to the cat, as he had to the moor when he first arrived at Biggnaherry. He wanted to find out who she was. The cat retreated.

'Stay,' he meowed. 'I want to thank you.' He took another step. The cat didn't move. He took another, his heart pounding with excitement. He was going to meet a wildcat!

'Darling, where are you?' It was Mrs Cheddar.

'Atticus!' Mr Tucker's voice floated over the moor.

Atticus glanced behind. The search party was coming towards them with more torches.

'Over here!' shouted Inspector Cheddar.

'Sheeeeeeeeeeee!'

Atticus twisted round sharply.

'Sheeeeeeeeeeee!' The wildcat had seen the search party. With a whip of its tail it slunk behind the rock and was gone.

Atticus felt a tug round his tummy. Mr Tucker picked him up. The light of his torch fell on

Inspector Cheddar's bedsock. 'Hang on a minute, what's this stinker doing here?' Mr Tucker exclaimed. 'I'd best show Edna,' he said, tucking it into his trousers. 'Now let's get you inside, Atticus, where it's nice and cosy.'

Just for once Atticus didn't want to be nice and cosy. He wanted to be out on the moor and meet the mysterious wildcat who had saved his life. But he couldn't very well explain that to Mr Tucker, not now humans couldn't understand Cat any more. With a last look over his shoulder he allowed himself to be borne away back to the cottage.

Atticus slept in the next morning. He woke up to find Mimi tugging at his tail with her teeth.

'The humans have worked it out,' she said. 'They're about to make a plan. Hurry up!'

Downstairs in the kitchen Mrs Tucker was in her Hells Angels nightie and matching curlers, making mugs of hot chocolate with Bones. Don and Debs were playing a quick round of Heave the Haggis with Callie and Michael, Mr Tucker was smoking his fish pipe and Mrs Cheddar was ticking off lists on her clipboard.

Atticus gave Bones a wave. 'Thanks for getting help last night,' he meowed.

'You're welcome!' Bones meowed back, adding marshmallows to the steaming drinks. 'I had a job

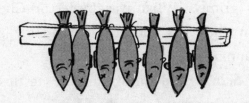

waking Mr Tucker – he'd put smokies in his ears so he didn't have to listen to Mrs Tucker snoring.'

'Where's Inspector Cheddar?' Atticus asked Mimi.

'He's hiding under Great-Uncle Archie's electric blanket,' Mimi said with a sigh. 'They're trading scary stories about cats.'

'What?' Atticus spluttered. 'Why's he doing that? He should be out arresting Lady Jemima for trying to kill him!'

'He doesn't believe the creature on the moor is a panther,' Mimi said. 'He thinks he had a near-death experience with the Cat Sith.'

'He's been listening to Great-Uncle Archie, unfortunately,' Bones explained. 'He's told Inspector Cheddar the wildcats have found out he's a Dumpling and sent the Cat Sith to warn him off the Roman gold.'

'More like Lady Jemima's found out!' said

Atticus grimly. 'What was Inspector Cheddar's reaction when Mrs Tucker told him Lady Jemima was planning to bulldoze the moor?'

'She didn't,' said Mimi, 'in case he tips Lady Jemima off that we've rumbled her.'

That was very sensible of Mrs Tucker, thought Atticus. Inspector Cheddar seemed incapable of identifying a villain even if they were standing in front of him with a sign round their neck saying 'I DID IT'.

'Oh, there you are, Atticus,' Mrs Tucker said. 'I think you already know about this.' She gestured at the kitchen table. The evidence was laid out on top of it. 'Could I have everyone's attention?' she hollered.

Everyone stopped what they were doing to listen.

'Will you make a list of the exhibits please, Mrs Cheddar?' said Mrs Tucker, holding them up one by one.

'Of course.' Mrs Cheddar wrote neatly on her clipboard.

<u>Exhibits in the Case of the Misty Moor</u>

- One smelly bedsock covered in drool belonging to Inspector Cheddar (the bedsock, not the drool)
- One wristwatch spy camera with photos of a plan to redevelop Biggnaherry Castle into a Las Vegas-style bingo joint
- One losing scratch card
- One diary belonging to Stewart Dumpling (deceased)

Mrs Tucker put the diary back on the table. 'All of these provide conclusive proof firstly that Lady Jemima Dumpling will stop at nothing to turn Biggnaherry moor into an indoor bingo park; and secondly that she is intent on concealing the truth by pretending that her pet panther is the Cat Sith.'

Everyone nodded glumly.

'It's disgusting,' said Debs. 'I'd like to knock her

block off with a cheese.' She pushed her sleeves up. To Atticus's interest he saw that she had another tattoo, which read:

WORLD CHEESE THROWING CHAMPION: HEAVYWEIGHT DIVISION

'Thanks, Debs; that's certainly one solution,' said Mrs Tucker. 'We'll come back to that. But first I'd like to thank our brilliant team of detectives for collecting the evidence. Michael identified the animal at the station as a panther; Herman sniffed out the sock; Callie took the photos; and Mimi and Bones zoomed in on the small print and showed it to me this morning.' She patted her curlers. 'I have no idea how we came to be in possession of the scratch card and the diary . . .' She looked sideways at Atticus. 'But I'm guessing it has something to do with a certain Police Cat Sergeant Claw?'

Atticus purred throatily. He'd got so wrapped up in the events on the moor last night he'd forgotten how much he liked being a cat detective, especially when Mrs Tucker was on the case.

'I thought so,' said Mrs Tucker. 'Good work, Atticus.' She glanced round the eager faces. 'Between us, I'm quite sure we can outsmart Lady Jemima, as long as Inspector Cheddar doesn't give us away. No offence,' she added to Mrs Cheddar.

'None taken,' Mrs Cheddar assured her.

Bones finished stirring the mugs of hot chocolate. Mrs Tucker handed them round. There was an unpleasant slurping noise.

'I's got maaaarrrrsshmallow stuck to me gum,' Mr Tucker explained, flicking his false teeth out and cleaning them on Inspector Cheddar's bedsock.

'Stop tampering with the evidence, Herman!' shouted Mrs Tucker.

'Sorry!' Mr Tucker put the sock down and used his beard-jumper instead. 'These maarrssshmallows are as sticky as a squashed jellyfish,' he complained.

Mrs Tucker ignored him. 'So, we're all agreed that Lady Jemima's plan stinks,' she said. 'The question is, what are we going to do about it? One option is for Debs to knock Lady Jemima's block off with a large cheese. The problem with that is that Debs will go to prison for the rest of her life. Has anyone got any other ideas?'

141

'Stop Lady Jemima finding the treasure,' said Michael. 'Then she can't do anything to the moor.'

'I'm afraid it might be too late for that,' Mrs Tucker said. 'The way I read it, she must be close or she wouldn't be so desperate to keep people away with the panther.'

'Does it tell you where the treasure is in the diary?' asked Don.

'I don't think so. Not in so many words anyway,' said Mrs Tucker. 'Which means she must have a knockout Plan B, like we have with Debs and the cheese.'

A knockout Plan B. Atticus hadn't thought of that. But it sounded plausible. Lady Jemima was desperate to get her hands on the treasure. If the diary didn't give away its location, she would find another way to unlock the secret. It suddenly struck Atticus that Lady Jemima's knockout Plan B might have something to do with Peregrine.

'I know what we should do,' said Callie. 'We should find the treasure before Lady Jemima does and hide it somewhere else.'

'I agree,' said Mrs Tucker. She picked up the diary. 'If Stewart Dumpling really did find the treasure, I reckon he would have left a clue in here. Maybe Lady Jemima's missed it. Now, concentrate, everyone.'

Atticus screwed his face into an attitude of rapt attention as Mrs Tucker opened the diary and began to read.

EXTRACTS FROM THE DIARY OF
STEWART RENNET DUMPLING

Tuesday 1st December, 1987

*I am Stewart Rennet Dumpling, Laird of Biggnaherry
Castle. I have decided to keep this diary to chronicle
my attempt (with my good friend Archibald McMucker
of Biggnaherry Cottage) to unlock the secret of the
Roman treasure of Biggnaherry moor. If, contrary to
my firm belief, there does exist upon the moor a
creature known as the Cat Sith, which has been
entrusted by the wildcats with the task of protecting
the treasure from the descendants of the Pictish
leader, Domplagan, then in all likelihood, if you are*

reading this now, I will be dead. In any event, it is my intention to set down everything we discover for future generations of Dumplings so that they may decide for themselves as to whether there is any truth in the story of the Dumpling family curse . . .

<u>Friday 4th December</u>
Archie and I have searched the castle from top to bottom with no luck so far. From now on we are going to concentrate the search on the cellars. We think that is where Domplagan would most likely have hidden the gold if he defeated the Roman legion in battle. But the cellars are extensive. Some of the excavations date back to when the castle was first built. Many of the chambers are bricked up and others have passages and tunnels that lead only to dead ends. Archie and I have resolved to make a map, so that we can find our way through the labyrinth. We start tomorrow.

<u>Monday 7th December</u>
Today is another dull and foggy day with the threat of rain. It is seldom it doesn't rain here upon the moor. The last sunny day I can remember was June 27th

1976, the day dear wee Jemima was born. What a gem she is, especially precious to me since her mother left on a one-way ticket to Australia. But then she is a Dumpling and all Dumplings are stout and loyal of heart. The dear girl is always busy, finding things about the castle to amuse her during the long dark days of winter. She shows a particular interest in wildlife television programmes about big cats and is often to be found in the attic playroom making bingo cards. I fcel blessed to have her as a daughter and to know that the future of the moor is safe in her hands.

Talking of which, there is a big storm brewing on the moor. I must remember to tell dear Jemima to keep the draughts out from under the duvet tonight.

Wednesday 9th December
The storm was the worst I have ever experienced. I fear our search for the Roman treasure may be doomed to failure. Archie and I will have our work cut out chopping up fallen trees and pumping water from the cellars into the loch before we can start again.

Dear Jemima has offered to help but I have sent her up to the playroom to amuse herself. She tells me she is putting on a one-girl play which she has written to keep our spirits up, entitled 'When I am Rich'! She asks me if she may dress up in the Dumplings' old frocks and furs, of which there are many. (Most of them belonged to Lord Hilary Blair Deuteronomy Dumpling, the old rascal!) I see no reason why not – I do not plan to wear them myself – and I have given her my old school trunk to put them in. That trunk was a present from my own father when I went to boarding school. It has a secret drawer for hiding tuck which has a rather interesting mechanism to open it, although I shall not trouble dear Jemima with that as she is only a little girl and may find it difficult to operate.

Now, on with the chopping and mopping, say I, so that Archie and I may resume our hunt for the treasure.

Thursday 10th December
I can scarcely believe it! Today Archie and I struck gold when we least expected to. As we went about

clearing the debris from the storm, we came across a secret tunnel beside the loch at the roots of a fallen tree.

We crawled through the tunnel, fearing that we should never again see the light of day. Eventually, after many wrong turns, we stumbled upon a chamber buried deep below the earth. Full it was of beetles and bugs and hung with white cobwebs as thick as the mist upon the moor. Somehow we found the courage to push our way through them and there, in the middle of the floor, a heavy stone was embedded in the earth. It took the two of us to jemmy it open, using an old iron tool that we found beside it. But at last we managed to move it a fraction. Enough to see that the stone concealed a deep pit and within the pit lay the Roman treasure.

Mountains of precious coins shimmered in the torchlight like sand dunes made of gold, and upon them, within touching distance, sat the terrifying standard of the Roman eagle, its eyes gazing blindly back at us in the torchlight.

What joy we experienced when first we clapped eyes on it, what wealth it promised . . .

And yet after all this I find I am forbidden by an oath from revealing the precise whereabouts of the treasure. It must remain buried for the time being at least.

You see, poor Archie has become increasingly worried over the last few days that the legend of the Cat Sith may be true after all. He does not fear for himself, you understand – because he is a McMucker not a Dumpling – but for me. For today when we came out of the tunnel we saw a wildcat. It stood upon the moor beside the loch, watching our every move. Archie is becoming superstitious. He thinks it's a sign; a sign that the Highland Tigers have been spying on us. He believes it meant to warn us off, and that if we don't leave the treasure alone the wildcats will gather as a clan and summon the Cat Sith against me.

Archie was so upset I was forced to make a promise. I agreed that we would hide our treasure map for a period of one year. If in that time nothing happens to me, then we will know that the legend of the Cat Sith was simply a myth. If, on the other hand, I die an untimely and suspicious death, then the treasure should remain buried to prevent any other Dumpling from suffering from the curse that haunts this family.

Of course I argued with Archie. I told him that were I to die in the next twelve months, it would be a mere accident. Besides, I said, the wildcats have nothing to fear from me. I intend to use the money to make a sanctuary for them so that the rift betwen our two kinds may be at an end.

But Archie held the trump card. He reminded me of my daughter, dear Jemima. If there were the smallest chance the legend was true, he said, and I was to die at the paws of the Cat Sith, then I would not wish the same fate on my dearest child. She might be in jeopardy if I was to claim the gold. It is possible that no Dumpling would be safe for evermore.

I felt obliged to comply with his demands. I would not risk sweet innocent Jemima's life for anything. It is better that she lives in a leaky castle with bedsocks to keep out the draughts under the duvet than chance the wrath of the Cat Sith, were it to truly exist. With this in mind I agreed that we should wait one year. If at the end of that time I am still in good health then I will claim the treasure and create the sanctuary of which I dream.

Then came the business of what we should do with the treasure map. Archie was all for destroying it but I refused. Without the map, I said, the secret would remain with the wildcats and our search would have been for nothing.

Archie finally saw the sense in this and gave way, but on condition that the hiding place for the map is completely secure. Both of us have to be present to open it. He insisted on this, he told me, for my own sake, because he does not wish me to give way to temptation and go back on my oath.

I struggled to think of such a hiding place but finally it came to me in a flash of inspiration. Whilst Jemima was at dinner, the two of us crept through the castle and solemnly locked the map away. It has fallen to me to guard the lock while Archie is to be the keeper of the key.

And there the matter rests, dear diary, for the next twelve months. Now I am off to watch Jemima's play.

<u>Friday 11th December</u>
I had little sleep last night. I had no idea dear Jemima wished so ardently to be rich! The way she paraded in Hilary Blair Deuteronomy's frocks and furs! The places she wishes to travel! Who'd have thought Las Vegas would be top of her list? She is next in line to the Dumpling fortune and she has a right to know where the treasure lies. In the event, I could have created a sanctuary for the wildcats AND given Jemima everything she wanted, had I the courage to seize the gold.

I am in a quandary, tormented by the thought that if I do die in the next twelve months Jemima will not be able to benefit from what Archie and I have discovered, but I am bound by my oath to Archie not to breathe a word to anyone.

And yet, and yet I do not think I shall break my pledge to my dear friend if I leave a riddle for Jemima as to the whereabouts of the treasure map. She is the next in line to the Dumpling fortune and – although I pray not – to the curse, if it is real. It seems to me she has a right to know where the treasure lies and in the event of my death it should be for her to decide if she wishes to take the risk of claiming it herself. It is a hard riddle, but one that I feel she is sure to decipher when she is older from the clues contained in this account.

> One to lock, another to open,
> Until then not a word be spoken,
> Pretend to be what you want to be,
> For that's when the Cat Sith holds the key.

Now I need to clear my head. So it's off to the iced-over loch for me to practise skinny-dipping ready for our traditional celebrations at Hogmanay.

18

There was silence for a moment when Mrs Tucker finished reading.

'So they did find the treasure,' said Callie eventually.

'And Great-Uncle Archie made Lord Stewart promise to wait before he claimed it in case the legend of the Cat Sith was true,' said Michael.

Just because he saw a wildcat! thought Atticus indignantly. Atticus wished he could prove to Great-Uncle Archie that cats were good, not bad. All the wildcats wanted was to protect their habitat.

Atticus didn't believe they would ever hurt anyone, except the original Domplagan perhaps, but that served him right.

'If only Looorrrrd Stewart hadn't gone skinny-dipping in the freezing-cold loch,' observed Mr Tucker, sucking away at his pipe. 'Then the mooooooor would have been safe from Lady Jemima.'

'To think he planned to turn it into a sanctuary for the wildcats,' Don said with a sigh. 'What a shame he didn't get the chance!'

Atticus agreed. *Then the Roman gold would have been spent on something worthwhile and the wildcats wouldn't have to worry any more.*

'And now look!' Debs scowled.

'At least Lady Jemima didn't solve the riddle,' Mrs Cheddar said cheerfully. 'Or she'd have found the map and turned the moor into a bingo park years ago.'

Mrs Tucker looked around the kitchen at the eager faces of her team of helpers. 'The question is, can *we* solve it?' she said. 'Thinking caps on, everyone.'

'Please can you read it again, Mrs Tucker?' Callie asked.

Atticus concentrated hard. He hadn't solved a

riddle before but he was sure he'd be good at it – he was good at everything else.

'Here goes.' Mrs Tucker found the place in the diary.

> *One to lock, another to open,*
> *Until then not a word be spoken,*
> *Pretend to be what you want to be,*
> *For that's when the Cat Sith holds the key.*

Atticus's chewed ear drooped. What on earth was it about? He looked at Mimi for inspiration.

'Shhhh!' she said. 'I'm thinking.'

Silence descended on the kitchen. Atticus tried to engage his brain but all he could hear was the kitchen clock ticking, like on a TV game show.

It was Michael who got the first part. 'The diary said Lord Stewart would guard the lock and Great-Uncle Archie would keep the key. So "one to lock" must be Lord Stewart and "another to open" is Great-Uncle Archie.'

'Well done, Michael!' Mrs Tucker offered him another marshmallow as a reward.

Atticus wondered if Mrs Tucker would give *him*

a smokie if he got any of the riddle right. He decided to try harder.

Debs got the next bit. '"Until then not a word be spoken" – that means the two of them promised one another they would keep the hiding place a secret until they opened it together.'

Oh yes, thought Atticus. He'd get the hang of it in a minute.

'Good, Debs.' Mrs Tucker nodded. 'Now we're getting somewhere. What about the next part? "Pretend to be what you want to be . . ."'

This bit was really hard. Atticus groomed his whiskers thoughtfully.

'Is it to do with the stage?' suggested Mrs Cheddar.

'What do you mean, Mum?' asked Callie.

'Well, if you're an actor you pretend to be someone else. Lady Jemima wrote a play called *When I am Rich*. That was what she wanted to be more than anything: rich.'

Drat! Atticus could see it now. Everyone else apart from him was so good at riddles he was beginning to feel quite annoyed.

'She dressed up in old Hilary Blairrrrrr

Deuteronomy's frocks and fuuurrrrrs,' Mr Tucker observed.

'That's it!' Callie exclaimed suddenly. 'The dressing-up box! Lord Stewart gave Lady Jemima his old school trunk to use as a dressing-up box!'

'The trunk had a secret drawer!' Michael remembered. His face split into a broad grin. 'Callie's right, Mrs Tucker. The treasure map must be in there!'

Mrs Tucker whistled. She handed the packet of marshmallows to the children and Mr Tucker to finish. 'Holy hake! You've cracked it, you three!'

Atticus couldn't help feeling a tiny bit jealous. He was rubbish at riddles. He'd never get that smokie now.

Mrs Tucker was still speaking. 'It makes perfect sense. Lord Stewart kept the trunk at the castle with the map hidden inside it and gave the key to the secret drawer to Great-Uncle Archie . . .'

'And Lady Jemima never suspected a thing!' Debs snorted.

Mrs Tucker looked expectantly at Don. 'So where's the key?'

'That's the problem,' Don said. 'I've never seen

a key in Great-Uncle Archie's room.' He turned to Debs. 'Have you, Debs?'

Debs shook her head. 'Never.'

'Could he have hidden it?' asked Mrs Tucker.

'I don't think so,' said Don. 'Debs and I check every inch of that room for cats six times a day. We'd have seen it if it was there.'

'What's the last line of the riddle again, Mrs Tucker?' asked Callie. 'Maybe that will give us a clue.'

Atticus listened sourly. There was barely any point in *him* trying to work it out when everyone else was so good at it.

'For that's when the Cat Sith holds the key.'

There was a long silence.

'I don't get it,' said Michael.

'Me neither,' Callie said, sounding disappointed. 'It's supposed to be Great-Uncle Archie who holds the key, not the Cat Sith.'

What did the Cat Sith have to do with it? Atticus didn't get it either. But that was hardly surprising, he thought crossly, given how useless he was at solving riddles compared to everyone else.

'Atticus.' Mimi's paw brushed his fur. 'Remember

in the diary it said the secret drawer had an interesting mechanism to open it? What does that actually mean? Do you know?'

Atticus thought back to his cat-burgling days. 'Not all locks have metal keys,' he told Mimi. 'Some are much trickier to break. Take a safe, for instance: that might have a combination of numbers or a dial.'

'What other types of key are there?' Mimi persisted.

'Computer codes, finger-print detectors, magnetic strips, symbols . . .'

'Symbols?' Mimi echoed.

'You know, like a jigsaw puzzle, where one piece fits inside another and it releases the lock . . .' Atticus stopped. That was it! A symbol. Now he understood where the Cat Sith fitted into the riddle. And he knew exactly where to find the key. His green eyes glowed. It turned out he was brilliant at riddles after all! Just like everyone else. He planted a lick on Mimi's cheek. 'Thanks, Mimi!'

'What for?' asked Mimi.

'I know where the key is. Stay here. I'll go and get it.'

Atticus raced out of the kitchen and up the stairs to Great-Uncle Archie's bedroom. The door was ajar. Two voices drifted through the gap.

'Ah told you at the station it was comin',' Great-Uncle Archie said. 'And ya wouldn't listen.'

'I wish I had!' came Inspector Cheddar's anguished reply. 'It was horrible, a real brute of a thing. Do you think I'll be safe under the electric blanket?'

'Ah doubt it,' said Great-Uncle Archie gloomily. 'No Dumpling is ever safe from the Cat Sith. It creeps up on you like a pair of tight underpants. Let's watch *Highlanders*, it's ma favourite soap opera. It'll take your mind off things.'

Atticus heard a click, then some dreary music, then lots of people shouting at one another.

161

He crept through the door.

Great-Uncle Archie sat in a tartan armchair by the window with a tartan blanket over his knees. He was wearing tartan pyjamas, tartan slippers, tartan socks, a tartan cardigan and, most probably, tartan underpants (although luckily you couldn't see those). Inspector Cheddar lay on the bed. Atticus couldn't actually tell what the Inspector was wearing because he was sandwiched between the mattress and a stiff pink blanket with wires coming out of it attached to a plug. Only Inspector Cheddar's face was visible. It gleamed ghost-like in the dark room, illuminated by the light from the TV. Even though it was mid-morning, the windows were closed and the heavy curtains pulled.

The room was also unbearably hot. Great-Uncle Archie had the radiator turned up to MAX and the electric blanket to MEGA-MAX. Sweat ran down Inspector Cheddar's face. Atticus couldn't help feeling a bit sorry for him. But then again, thought Atticus, it was perfectly obvious to anyone who had an ounce of sense that the animal on the moor wasn't the Cat Sith, but Lady Jemima's pet panther.

'Stop mumbling!' Great-Uncle Archie shook his

fist at the TV and turned the volume up to SUPER-MEGA-MAX. The shouting became deafening. Great-Uncle Archie and Inspector Cheddar were glued to the screen.

Now was his chance. Atticus's eyes swept the room. He found what he was looking for almost immediately: Stewart Dumpling's walking stick. It stood upright against Great-Uncle Archie's commode in the corner beside the dressing table. Atticus had to admire the two men's deception. Great-Uncle Archie didn't *need* to hide the key because no one (except now Atticus, of course) knew that was what the walking stick actually was.

Atticus edged along the skirting board, hoping that the faded flock wallpaper would camouflage him. He reached the walking stick and prodded at it tentatively with a paw, wondering how he was going to get it out of the room without Inspector Cheddar seeing him. The walking stick was made of solid oak. That, combined with the silver knob, made it far too heavy for Atticus to carry.

He would have to roll it.

CRASH! BANG! '*@$@$%*! *@©†Ωπ₡ €∫ ‰ž
$%@&@*! $%&*@†Ωπ₡$%&*! @$*@©†Ωπ₡
$*@©†Ωπ₡$%&*@$%! &*@$%&*@$%&*@$
%&*@$%&! *@$%&* €∫ ‰ž†Ωπ₡%& *@$%&*
@$%&*@$% &*@$%&*@$€∫ †Ωπ₡‰ž* @$%
&*@$%& *@ €∫ ‰ ž@$%&*@$%†Ωπ₡!'

The argument on the TV intensified.

Atticus seized his opportunity. He pulled the walking stick away from the commode with a quick tug of his front paws. It dropped on to the carpet with a thud. Luckily the carpet was thick – the noise was lost against the shouts of the quarrelling Highlanders. As quickly as he could, Atticus rolled the walking stick out of the room and along the corridor.

TWING! CLATTER-CLATTER-CLATTER! TWING!
CLATTER-CLATTER-CLATTER! TWING!

The walking stick bounced down the stairs, knocking against the banisters. With a final heave Atticus pushed it through the kitchen door.

Seven pairs of human eyes regarded him blankly.

'What are you doing with that, Atticus?' Mrs Tucker inquired.

164

Atticus planted his front paws on the tiled floor and manoeuvred the walking stick with his strong hind legs until the silver knob was turned in the direction of the humans. The shape of the Cat Sith stood out bold and clear, as did Stewart Dumpling's initials.

Atticus waited patiently for the penny to drop.

Mimi was the first to get it. 'You are clever, Atticus,' she said. 'I'd never have guessed that part of the riddle.'

'That's because you weren't a cat burglar.' Atticus felt proud of himself. If only the humans would hurry up and work it out! He gave the walking stick another nudge.

'Maybe he wants to go for a walk?' suggested Debs.

Atticus took a deep breath. He wasn't a dog, for goodness' sake!

'You'll have to show them,' Mimi said.

'Okay.' Atticus flicked out a claw and pretended to pick a lock.

'It's like charrrrrraaaaarrrrrrrrdes.' Mr Tucker clapped his hands in delight. Atticus cradled the silver knob in his paws and twisted it gently so that the symbol of the Cat Sith turned one way and the other. Then he put his paw to his ear as if he were listening for a click. Then he opened an imaginary drawer. Surely they'd get it now!

'I know!' A smile lit Callie's face.

'Know what?' asked Don.

'You tell them,' Callie said to her brother. Michael was grinning too.

'The walking stick,' said Michael. 'That's it, isn't it, Atticus?'

Atticus meowed.

'That's what?' asked Debs.

'The key!' The children chorused.

'So that's why Great-Uncle Archie wouldn't part with it all these years!' Don whistled. 'I should have guessed.'

'Good work, Atticus.' Mrs Tucker smiled. 'I think you deserve a smokie for that.' She went to the fridge.

'I'll share it with you,' Atticus promised Mimi, 'because you helped.'

Mrs Tucker placed a saucer of fish on the floor. Atticus gulped down his treat. Mimi had a bit too. And Bones.

166

'Now let's go and get that treasure map,' said Mrs Tucker, pulling on her biker boots and tying a Hells Angels scarf over her curlers. 'There's no time to lose.'

'I'll write Dad a note,' Callie said, 'in case he wonders where we are.'

'All right,' Mrs Tucker said, 'but don't tell him what we're doing.'

'I won't.' Callie scribbled something quickly and pinned it to the pegboard.

'What are we going to say to Lady Jemima?' asked Michael, as the kids grabbed their coats and wellies.

Mrs Tucker gave him a wink. 'How about we ask if you and Callie can borrow some costumes for the Hogmanay party from the dressing-up trunk?'

20

On Biggnaherry moor, Thug and Slasher emerged from their morning paddle in the freezing-cold loch. Drops of water dripped from their bedraggled feathers on to the stony beach.

The castle loomed behind them on the hill. It was just about visible through the thick fog.

'What a horrible place to live.' Thug shivered.

'It's an 'orrible place for an 'orrible person,' said Slasher, referring to Lady Jemima.

'Oh, *her*!' said Thug in disgust. 'I can't

believe she's planning to feed us to a panther when we've done the job.'

'I can!' said Slasher. 'She's a human. All humans are 'orrible. Like what Jimmy said. You can't trust 'em.'

'When do we start spreading the word?' Thug asked. He nodded meaningfully at the loch. The other members of the Crow Brigade were still splashing about energetically doing birdy-fly.

'Not yet,' Slasher said. 'We have to wait until Jimmy gives the order. We need to find the treasure first, remember?'

'Oh yeah,' Thug said. The thought of treasure cheered him a little. 'Hey, Slash, whatchergonna do with your share when you get back to Littleton-on-Sea?'

'I'm gonna get myself a new nest to put it in,' said Slasher, 'then I'm gonna hire the Crow Brigade to kill Atticus Claw.'

'You mean you're leaving our nest under the pier?' gasped Thug.

'Nah, I'm not leaving it. I want to put the gold next door so I can go and look at it whenever I want. What about you?'

'I'm gonna get a tail extension,' said Thug.

He and Slasher fell to chattering about the future.

'Chacka-chacka-chacka-chacka-chacka!'

'Chacka-chacka-chacka-chacka-chacka!'

Unfortunately the noise attracted the attention of the Sergeant Major. 'Time for your rub-down with the prickly sock!' he shouted.

'Darn it!' said Thug.

The prickly socks (so named because they were full of thistles) were lined up on the beach, one for each member of the Crow Brigade. The drill involved the recruits rubbing their feathers against the rough, prickly wool until they were completely dry.

'What's the point of it, anyway?' grumbled Thug, picking the least prickly sock he could find. 'I mean, why can't we just use a towel?'

'It's good for your circul-hation,' said Slasher.

'But I've got sensitive skin,' said Thug, easing his tail gently against the toe of the sock.

'Too bad!' The Sergeant Major gave him a shove.

'OUCH!' Thug sat back on the sock. A large thistle head shot through a hole in the toe and spiked him painfully in the backside.

'Fall in!' shouted the Sergeant Major.

The other members of the Crow Brigade finished their rub-down and sprang into a neat line.

'Make room for us!' Thug and Slasher pushed their way in.

'Atten-*shun!*'

The birds stood tall and erect.

'That includes you two!' yelled the Sergeant Major. 'Stop slouching!'

'I'm not!' Thug insisted. 'I'm just shorter than everyone else.'

'And I'm lopsided because of my Arthur-itis,' Slasher said, leaning on Thug.

'Okay, you two, have it your way.' The Sergeant Major's face wore an unpleasant smirk.

'Why's he being so nice all of a sudden?' Slasher asked a neighbouring jay.

'Haven't you heard?' said the jay. 'The Wing Commander's on his way. If you don't fall into line he'll mince you and save the Sergeant Major a job. I'd watch it if I were you.' He nodded towards the castle. 'Here he comes now with the other officers.'

A perfect V-shaped formation of birds flew low over the moor. It zoomed over the heads of the recruits in a brilliant display of aerobatics.

'There's Jimmy!' cried Thug in excitement.

Jimmy Magpie flew just behind and to the right of the Wing Commander. Only centimetres separated him from the bird flying on the Wing Commander's left flank.

'That's awesome!' Slasher said.

'Prepare to land!' screeched the Wing Commander.

One by one the pairs of birds veered off in opposite directions, landing with perfect precision at either end of the line of recruits. Jimmy and his flying partner were the last pair to land. They put down together at exactly the same time.

'Hey, Boss!' Thug waved. 'Over here!'

Jimmy marched up to Thug and punched him smartly in the crop. 'Shut up, you idiot,' he hissed.

'You're not supposed to speak to me. Don't say anything else if you want to get out of here alive.' He stepped back into place.

'Uuuuuuuuuuu.' Thug inhaled a great ragged breath. He couldn't have said anything anyway, even if he had wanted to, which was probably just as well because a terrible screech heralded the arrival of the bird they had all been waiting for – the Wing Commander.

The recruits looked up.

A huge bird with a blue-grey head and a cruel, hooked blue-and-yellow beak plummeted from the sky. At the very last minute it pulled itself up in front of the Crow Brigade and beat its white spotted wings in the faces of the recruits. The line of birds shuffled backwards in fear.

'Stand your ground!' the bird ordered. 'Or I'll peck your eyes out.'

The recruits froze, apart from Thug and Slasher whose knees knocked together like two pairs of maracas.

The bird stalked slowly up and down the line, its beady eyes unblinking. Finally it stopped.

'I'm Wing Commander Peregrine

Falcon,' it said. 'I'm the commanding officer of this brigade.' Peregrine rotated his head full circle one way, then the other, keeping all the recruits within sight.

'Congratulations,' he continued. 'Most of you have passed the training course with flying colours. Thanks to the Sergeant Major, you have been transformed from a bunch of cut-throat ruffians into a mean, lean fighting machine.' Peregrine's eyes fell on Thug and Slasher. 'Two of you, however, are useless. It's only thanks to Squadron Leader Magpie that you are still alive. He believes you might come in useful for carrying supplies.' Peregrine regarded Thug and Slasher with contempt. 'Personally I think you're about as much use as a dose of bird flu, so watch your step or I'll crush you with my toes. Got it?'

'Got it,' Thug and Slasher gulped.

'The rest of you listen up.' Peregrine resumed his pacing. 'You have been trained for a particular mission, which I shall refer to as Plan B. If you succeed, you'll get paid with something shiny. If you fail, you'll die. If you tell any-birdy else, I'll tear you into shreds and feed you to the eagles. Understood?'

'Yes, sir! Understood, sir!' the Corvids chorused.

'Very well,' said the falcon. 'Here it is, then – Plan B. Your mission is to capture a wildcat and take it to the castle.'

There was a collective gasp, except from Thug. Peregrine's eyes swept the line. 'Pretend to be shocked,' Slasher hissed. 'We're not supposed to know the plan, remember?'

'Oh yeah!' Thug pressed his wings to his cheeks. 'Not a wildcat!' he sobbed. 'Oh no! Oh no! What will become of me?'

Peregrine silenced him with a look. 'My officers and I have already identified the location of the nearest wildcat's den.' He scratched out a map on the pebbles. 'It lies here, on the moor not far from Biggnaherry Cottage, beneath the ridge of rocks. It is vital, I repeat, vital, that the humans at the cottage do not get wind of our plan or they may try to stop us.' He waited for a moment to let this sink in.

'Yeah, humans stink,' Thug said with feeling.

'Shhhh!' Slasher clapped a wing over his beak. 'He's working for one, remember?'

'The wildcat is nocturnal,' Peregrine resumed.

'We will gather in the trees whilst it's asleep. As dusk falls I will lead my officers in an airborne attack, which will drive our quarry out of its den. Then on the command of the Sergeant Major you will bungee jump out of the trees and drop the net on top of it.'

'What net?' asked Thug.

'The one that you two are going to carry,' screamed Peregrine, 'along with the rest of the equipment.'

'All right, keep your beak on!' Thug said rudely.

Luckily Peregrine didn't hear. 'Half of you will then subdue the wildcat with prickly socks whilst the other half tie it up with your bungee ropes. Any questions?'

'How will we get it back to the castle, sir?' asked the Sergeant Major.

'Each bird will be issued with a strap,' Peregrine replied. 'Once the wildcat has been subdued, you will attach your strap to the net and airlift the wildcat back to the castle. Once it is safely imprisoned I shall take over with the other officers.'

'What do we do then, sir?' asked the Sergeant Major.

'Wait in the cellars to receive payment. Then you will be free to go.'

'Liar, liar, feathers on fire!' chanted Thug under his breath. 'We're all going to cop it.'

'Shhhh!' Slasher clapped the other wing over his beak.

Peregrine looked at the sky. It was early afternoon on the moor and in winter that meant that dusk wasn't far away. 'It's time to get ready,' he said. 'Follow me.'

21.

Back at Biggnaherry Castle, Lady Jemima Dumpling was on the phone in the hall to the landlord of the local pub. 'She's put on buses, did you say? So that everyone from the village can come to the Hogmanay party after all? How absolutely murderous – I mean marvellous. How many of you? Fifty-seven! Blast you! I mean – bless you! You'll bring the haggis for the heave the heavy haggis

competition? You're such a little wart, I mean such a good sport! It's a terrible line. See you on Friday, then. Goodbye! Goodbye! Good riddance!'

Lady Jemima threw the telephone at the wall. It smashed into pieces. Peregrine would be cross with her for losing her temper, but Peregrine wasn't there. He was out on the moor putting knockout Plan B into action. 'It's just as well Peregrine's got it covered,' said Lady Jemima to no one in particular. 'I need to find the treasure before those busybodies turn up on my doorstep again. Now, where *did* I put Daddy's diary?' Lady Jemima had been looking for it all day. 'I'm sure I left it on the coffee table in the drawing room.' She wrapped her cardigan around her and headed for the stairs.

KNOCK! KNOCK! KNOCK!

'Curses! What is it now?' Lady Jemima went to answer the door. She took a quick look at her reflection in the mirror. 'Aargh!' she jumped back in horror. 'I look about forty!' (Actually, Lady Jemima *was* about forty but for some reason she thought that *looking* about forty was a bad thing, which is why she had spent so much of her money on plastic surgery.) She massaged the face filler back into place and applied some lipstick.

KNOCK! KNOCK! KNOCK!

'I'M COMING, DAMMIT!' she roared. She pulled the door open with a vicious tug.

On the doorstep stood three cats, two children, the man with the wooden leg and the hairy jumper (or was it a beard? – she still couldn't decide), the woman with the basket and biker boots and the other one with the clipboard. (And Don and Debs.) The only one missing – and thank goodness for that because he was so boring she thought she'd die if she ever met him again – was the policeman who claimed to be her long-lost cousin, two hundred times removed. And Lady Jemima had a pretty good idea why he hadn't turned up! *Curses!* If only the rest of them were so easy to shake off . . .

'Not you again?' she snarled.

'What was that?' asked Mrs Tucker.

'I mean how lovely to see you again! What can I do for you this time?'

'We'd like to borrow some costumes please,' said Callie, 'so that we can dress up for the Hogmanay party.'

Lady Jemima eyed her suspiciously. She was a pretty little girl, but Lady Jemima didn't like little girls whether they were pretty or not. She didn't like little boys either, for that matter; or cats (except big ones like Chomper); or men with hairy jumpers and sporrans who had wooden legs, cooked stew and heaved haggis; or women with tattoos, baskets, and clipboards who mended roofs, threw cheese, had jobs as secret agents and went round organising parties people didn't want.

In fact, Lady Jemima didn't really like anyone except herself. And Peregrine. When she got round to bulldozing the moor in a couple of weeks' time and building the bingo park, she would make sure to keep one of the

hotels just for the two of them. 'Is that it?' she asked sourly. 'Just the costumes?'

'We can go through the arrangements for the party if you like?' Mrs Cheddar offered with a smile of such sweetness Lady Jemima thought she might be sick. How could people be so perfectly NICE? There should be a law against it.

'No thanks.' Lady Jemima glared at Mrs Cheddar. 'It sounds like you've got it all under control.'

'Right, just the costumes please,' said Mrs Tucker briskly, 'and then we'll be off.'

'Oh, very well,' Lady Jemima agreed. Anything to get rid of them before Peregrine got back with the wildcat! She didn't want them mucking up her knockout Plan B. 'There are some old frocks and furs in the attic. They're in the dressing-up box. Don and Debs can show you.'

'We'll use the back stairs,' Don said, leading the little group towards the kitchen.

Lady Jemima watched them file past. Her eyes narrowed. They all looked tricky, she decided, but the trickiest one was definitely the tabby cat. She didn't like his stripy fur, or his red handkerchief, or

his four white socks, or his fancy name, or his chewed ear, or the fact that he was the world's greatest cat detective. A thought struck her. The tabby was the last one in the drawing room yesterday when she was trying to shoo everyone else out. *Maybe he had something to do with the disappearance of Daddy's diary?*

'Hang on a minute,' she said.

The procession stopped.

'You didn't happen to see a little black book in the drawing room yesterday, did you?' she asked Mrs Cheddar.

'I don't think so,' said Mrs Cheddar. 'Did anyone else?'

The kids shook their heads. 'Dad had his notebook,' said Callie. 'Is that what you mean?'

'No,' Lady Jemima snapped. She wasn't sure whether to believe them or not. Were they covering for the cat? Had he swiped it when she wasn't looking? She needed to be sure they didn't suspect she was after the treasure. No one must know until the bulldozers moved in and it was too late to save the moor.

'Where *is* dear Ian Larry Barry?' she asked.

'Hiding under Great-Uncle Archie's electric blanket,' said Mrs Tucker. 'He thinks he saw the Cat Sith last night when he was out practising for the cheese throwing competition.'

Ha! Lady Jemima couldn't resist a smile. At least she wouldn't be seeing any more of *him*.

'Which is why we'd better hurry.' Mrs Cheddar put her hands on the children's shoulders and steered them towards the kitchen. 'We don't want to be out on the moor after dark in case the Cat Sith strikes again!'

Ha! Ha! Lady Jemima's smile broadened. They were *all* scared of the Cat Sith! Not just Ian Larry Barry.

'Definitely not,' Mrs Tucker agreed. She shook her head gravely. 'I thought it was just a story, but after what Inspector Cheddar saw last night, I'm totally convinced the Cat Sith is real.'

Ha! Ha! Ha! For the first time in ages, Lady Jemima felt like laughing. (She didn't actually laugh, just in case her face filler leaked out of her ears, but nevertheless she felt like it.) Even the secret agent had fallen for it! Cat detective or no cat detective, THE HUMANS DIDN'T SUSPECT A THING!

'Off you go, then,' she said merrily. 'Quick as you can! Chomp chomp . . . ! I mean, chop chop!' She pushed them into the kitchen and went back up the main stairs to resume her search for the diary. Not that it mattered very much whether she found it or not, Lady Jemima thought, rubbing her hands in glee. Once her visitors had gone it would be time to meet Peregrine and claim the Roman gold.

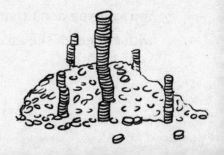

22

'Phew!' Mrs Tucker closed the attic door and leant against it with a sigh of relief. 'That was close! I thought she'd rumbled us when she asked about the diary.'

'Lucky youze didn't give anything away, Atticus,' Mr Tucker said, giving him a pat. 'I's didn't like the way she was lookin' at youze.'

Atticus didn't like it either. Lady Jemima looked like a waxwork in a horror film. It had been hard not to flinch when she fixed him with her lopsided stare.

'The cheek of the woman, asking where Inspector Cheddar was!' Debs scowled. 'When it was her who sent the panther to give him a fright! You sure you don't want me to knock her block off with a cheese?' she asked Mrs Cheddar wistfully.

'No, really, Debs, it's fine,' Mrs Cheddar assured her.

'It was a clever idea of Mum's and Mrs Tucker's to pretend that we're all frightened of the Cat Sith,' said Michael. 'Now Lady Jemima thinks none of us will go near the castle after dark. She won't have a clue we're looking for the treasure.'

'We'll have to be careful of the panther, though,' Don warned, 'in case she lets it out again.'

'I wonder where she keeps it,' said Callie.

Atticus was wondering that too. The cellars seemed the most likely place to keep a big cat hidden. And that was where the treasure was buried. Don was right – even though the Cat Sith was a fake, the panther was real. They would have to be very careful they didn't run into it by mistake.

'First things first,' said Mrs Tucker. 'Let's find that treasure map.'

'That must be the dressing-up box over there.' Callie pointed to the corner of the attic.

Stewart Dumpling's old school trunk was at the bottom of a mountain of junk. Dust flew everywhere as seven pairs of hands and three pairs of front paws dug their way through it. Bones was in charge of keeping everything ship-shape. She organised it all into neat piles so that there was space for everyone around the trunk.

'Best ship's cat ever is Bones,' Mr Tucker said proudly.

Atticus used to be jealous of Bones. But now he understood that different cats were good at different things. Bones was the best at organising; Mimi was the best at asking questions; and he was the best at being a cat detective (and burglar).

'Have you got Great-Uncle Archie's walking stick, Debs?' asked Mrs Tucker.

'Here.' Debs drew it out from under her long rain mac.

'So where's the secret drawer?' Everyone looked at Atticus expectantly.

'Maybe it's under all the dressing-up clothes.' Michael threw open the lid.

Atticus put his paws on the edge of the trunk and looked inside. Hilary Blair Deuteronomy's dusty frocks and furs had been shoved in any old how. They

188

looked as if they hadn't been touched since the day Lord Stewart drowned in the freezing-cold loch.

Atticus regarded the jumble of clothes thoughtfully. 'Mimi,' he meowed, 'can you remember what Stewart Dumpling kept in the secret drawer when he was at school?'

'Tuck,' replied Mimi.

'What's tuck?' asked Atticus.

'Food,' said Mimi.

'What sort of food?'

'Human treats – chocolate, sweets, cakes, that sort of thing.'

'Why did he have to hide it?'

'Because he wasn't allowed to take it to school,' said Mimi. 'Boarding schools were very strict in those days.'

'Thank you.' Atticus tried to imagine if he went to a boarding school and had a trunk where the best place would be to hide smokies. He would want to be able to get at them easily without taking everything else out first. 'I don't think it's under the frocks and furs,' he said. He dropped his front paws back to the floor and padded round the trunk.

The humans watched him carefully.

'What are you looking for?' Mimi asked Atticus.

'A picture of the Cat Sith,' Atticus replied, 'to fit the key into.'

'I can't see anything,' said Mimi, walking round the trunk in the other direction. 'Can you?'

'No. Ouch!' Atticus banged his head on the lid. He'd been concentrating so hard on the base of the trunk he'd forgotten that Michael had left the lid open.

He took a step back. *Aha!* The lid was about ten centimetres deep: a perfect place to conceal a secret drawer.

'It must be one of these,' he said. The lid was decorated all the way round with silver shields. Each shield was engraved with the Cat Sith. He felt round each one with his tail.

'Mind out, Atticus, it'll be easier if we close it.' Michael lifted the lid back into place.

Atticus had found the shield he was looking for. 'See this one?' he said to Mimi. 'The engraving is deeper than the others.'

'Oh yes!' said Mimi.

'Try it, Debs,' said Mrs Tucker.

Debs held Great-Uncle Archie's walking stick horizontally and fitted the silver knob into the shield.

'Now turn it.'

Debs twisted the walking stick gently to the left.

CLUNK! The mechanism of the lock sprang open. A crack appeared in the lid above the line of shields. Atticus ran his claws along it to make sure the wood didn't stick. Then Michael pulled open the secret drawer.

The treasure map lay face down on the bottom of the drawer. The paper was yellow and flaky. Mrs Tucker picked it up carefully so that it didn't disintegrate and placed it in a plastic folder that she had brought with her in her basket. Then she put it on the floor so that they could all see.

The map showed a maze of passages leading under the castle. Many of them were crossed off as dead ends but the route to the chamber where the treasure was buried was clearly shown.

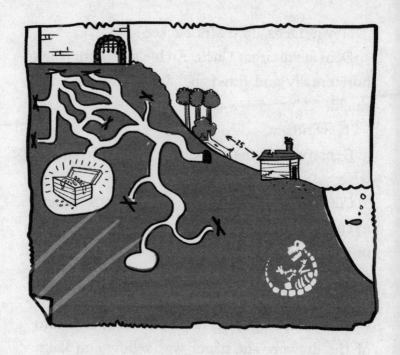

'Don, do you know where the entrance is?' asked Mrs Tucker. 'The diary said it was beside the loch.'

Don studied the treasure map carefully. The map showed a hut next to the water's edge, then a measurement in paces to the fallen oak tree. Behind the tree was the entrance to the labyrinth of tunnels.

'That's the boathouse,' he said, pointing to the hut.

'How do you get there?'

'From the castle you go through the basement and out of the cellars,' Don said. 'Or you can reach it by the back road by car. From there it's just a short walk through the woods down to the loch.'

'Right, then,' said Mrs Tucker, 'we'll take the jeeps and drive round so that Lady Jemima thinks we've gone back to the cottage. Then we'll lie low for a bit until it gets dark before we start the search. Do we have torches?'

'They're in the jeeps,' said Debs.

'Good, we'll need them.' Mrs Tucker put the map away in her basket. 'Callie, Michael, bring some dressing-up clothes in case we bump into Lady Jemima on the way down.'

Callie and Michael picked out two of Hilary Blair Deuteronomy's moth-eaten fur coats. Then Don led the way back down the stairs and out of the front door to the gravel drive.

'There she is.'

Atticus glanced up. Lady Jemima was watching them from the drawing-room window.

Mrs Tucker gave her a wave goodbye.

Lady Jemima waved back. Her face wore a broad smile.

Atticus felt anxious. There was still no sign of Peregrine. Where was he? Atticus hadn't seen the falcon all afternoon, yet the day before when they visited the castle Peregrine hadn't let Atticus out of his sight. And why was Lady Jemima smiling? Was it something to do with her maybe having a knockout Plan B like Mrs Tucker had suggested?

'Mimi,' he said, as they got back into the jeeps. 'If you were Lady Jemima and you couldn't work out the riddle, how else would you find the treasure?'

Mimi thought for a moment. 'I'd try to get someone who knew where it was to tell me.'

'But Great-Uncle Archie won't tell and there's no one else who knows . . .'

'There might be,' Mimi said slowly. 'If any part of the legend is true.'

'I don't follow,' Atticus said.

'Well,' said Mimi, 'usually with myths and legends, there's some basis in truth, even if most of it's made up.'

'Go on,' said Atticus.

'So even if there's no such thing as the Cat Sith, it doesn't mean that the wildcats didn't have anything to do with the disappearance of the treasure.'

'You mean it could have been them who hid the treasure when Domplagan turned against them?'

'Yes,' said Mimi, 'why not? They had everything to lose. Maybe they did it when he went off to battle again.'

'Do you think they still guard it?' Atticus said.

'Yes,' said Mimi simply. 'I think that's why the wildcat in the diary was watching Lord Stewart and Great-Uncle Archie. They know where it is, and they don't want any more Dumplings finding it.'

Atticus suddenly felt full of dread. Now he understood what Lady Jemima's knockout Plan B might be. She and Peregrine were going to force the wildcats to show them the way to the treasure.

23

Back at Biggnaherry Cottage, the bumper episode of *Highlanders* had finally ended. Inspector Cheddar was so hot under the electric blanket he thought he might faint. He was desperate for some fresh air and a drink of water.

Loud snoring from the wheelchair indicated that Great-Uncle Archie was fast asleep.

Inspector Cheddar got out from underneath the electric blanket. He tiptoed to the door. 'Darling,' he called to Mrs Cheddar in a loud whisper.

When there was no answer from Mrs Cheddar he tried again. 'Kids?' Still no answer. 'Mrs Tucker? Don? Debs? Mr Tucker?' Inspector Cheddar ran through the list. 'Atticus?' Inspector Cheddar gave up. Where was everyone? Suddenly a terrible

thought occurred to him. Perhaps they had all been eaten by the Cat Sith!

Inspector Cheddar dithered at the top of the stairs, wondering what horrors were below. Were they all lying dead in the kitchen? Had the Cat Sith carried them off across the moor? Could the electric blanket have saved him after all? Had the Cat Sith come for him but eaten his family instead? He felt racked with guilt. He had to know what had become of them, but he couldn't go down there unarmed, just in case the beast was lying in wait.

Inspector Cheddar tottered back into Great-Uncle Archie's room looking for a weapon. *Aha!* Upon the dressing table lay just what he was looking for: a packet of Thumpers' Traditional Cat Repellent. He picked it up and glanced at the instructions.

Got a problem with unwanted cats?
Are they pooing in your garden?
Are they scratching up your sofa?
Are they moulting on your bed?
Then Thumpers' Traditional Cat
Repellent is for you. Apply liberally to

affected areas and see the little beasts run for cover.

THUMPERS' TRADITIONAL

for all your cat repellent needs.
(Also works on mythical Cat Siths.)

Inspector Cheddar took the packet out on to the landing and shook it all over himself. He coughed and spluttered. Goodness, it stank a hundred times worse than his bedsocks! But it might hold off the Cat Sith long enough for him to rescue his family. Stuffing the half-empty packet into his trouser pocket, he crept down the stairs and into the kitchen. No one was there, but the mess on the table and the half-drained mugs of hot chocolate suggested they had left in a hurry.

On his way past the cooking range, Inspector Cheddar collected a large spatula and an iron frying pan. Very carefully he opened the back door and stuck his eye to the crack. The jeeps had gone. He felt a surge of relief. They had escaped. But how far would they get before the Cat Sith caught up with them? And where would they go? He wished they had left him a message.

Just then he saw a hastily scribbled note pinned to the pegboard. It was from Callie.

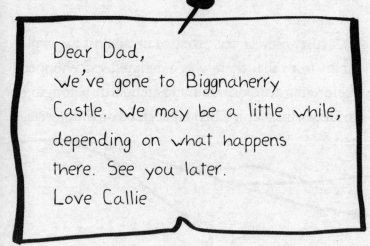

Dear Dad,
We've gone to Biggnaherry
Castle. We may be a little while,
depending on what happens
there. See you later.
Love Callie

Dear Callie! Inspector Cheddar felt a tear rise to his eye. She was so brave. And so were the others. They had fled to Biggnaherry Castle to warn Lady Jemima about the Cat Sith and very possibly to draw it away from *him*. Inspector Cheddar came to a decision. He stood up tall. He stuck out his chin in a policeman-like way and took a deep policeman-like breath. He had a duty to his family. He had a duty to the public. And he had a duty to Lady Jemima. They were the last two Dumplings of Biggnaherry and they should stick together to defeat this monster. He would go to the castle now and bash the Cat Sith before it ate anyone else. Clutching the spatula and the iron frying pan he crept out of the cottage in search of a means of transport.

A rusty bicycle was propped up against the wall. Apart from that there was a deflated spacehopper (belonging to Don) and a skateboard (belonging to Debs). Inspector Cheddar decided on the bicycle.

He glanced at the sky to see if he needed to switch his bicycle lamp on. Dusk was gathering. And so were a lot of birds. They were hanging out in a big flock in the trees beside the ridge of rock near where the Cat Sith had attacked him. Inspector Cheddar frowned. They were a nasty-looking lot – a bunch of ruffian crows and jays and jackdaws as far as he could make out. He looked harder. They seemed to be attaching hooks to the trees!

All of a sudden a cat broke cover from the rocks. It fled towards the trees, closely followed by a bird of prey and several other birds flying in close formation.

Atticus? Inspector Cheddar was almost sure it was his police cat sergeant the birds were chasing. It wasn't wearing a red handkerchief, but apart from that the resemblance was striking. What on earth was going on?

The cat had reached the trees. To Inspector Cheddar's amazement the roosting birds dropped

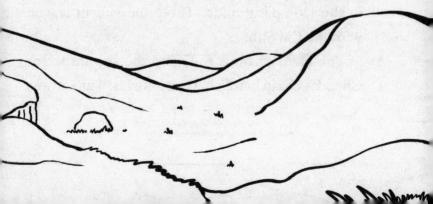

down from the branches on bungee ropes and threw something over the cat. It collapsed to the ground. The birds whizzed back up on the ropes, unhooked them from the tree and flew down to where the cat lay struggling. Inspector Cheddar couldn't quite see what happened next but it looked very much as if some of the birds were bashing at it with woolly socks whilst others used their bungee ropes to tie it up.

The bird of prey seemed to be the ringleader. It kept circling the others, screeching in a blood-curdling frenzy that Inspector Cheddar dimly recognised. Wait a minute! It was the same beastly bird that had knocked his torch out of his hand before the Cat Sith struck. It also dawned on him for the first time that it could be the same beastly bird that he'd seen in the drawing room at Biggnaherry Castle.

Peregrine!

Inspector Cheddar gasped. There was a traitor in the Dumpling midst. Peregrine was in league with the Cat Sith!

The team of birds rose into the sky. Inspector Cheddar could hardly believe his eyes. The cat was trussed up in the net. The birds were carrying it away with straps tied to their feet in the direction of Biggnaherry Castle.

Inspector Cheddar wasn't a police detective for nothing. He knew a catnapping when he saw one; and this wasn't any old catnapping. This was a catnapping of his police cat sergeant. Atticus must have escaped and tried to double back to warn him that the others were in danger. That's why the birds were rounding Atticus up: to take him to the Cat Sith under the watchful eye of that double-crossing imposter, Peregrine.

Well, he wasn't having that! No blasted bird was going to catnap his police cat sergeant. And no blasted Cat Sith was going to eat his family and friends. He, Ian Larry Barry Dumpling Cheddar, would make sure of that. Inspector Cheddar leapt on the bicycle and cycled furiously along the road after the vanishing birds.

Atticus felt restless. The jeeps were parked up under cover of woodland out of sight of the back road to the loch. The wait seemed to go on forever. 'Are you quite sure I shouldn't go and try to find Peregrine?' he asked Mimi.

'I'm sure,' said Mimi firmly. 'Think about it, Atticus: if you're right and Plan B means getting a wildcat to show him the way to the treasure, Peregrine will have to bring it here, to the castle. Your best chance of rescuing it is to be patient.'

Atticus knew she was right but it didn't make

the wait any easier. He wondered how Peregrine would force the wildcat to go with him. The falcon must have help, Atticus decided. *The panther, perhaps?* But even the panther had seemed wary of the wildcat. There must be more to Peregrine's knockout Plan B that he had yet to figure out.

'Okay,' Mrs Tucker said. 'I think we're ready.'

Atticus jumped out of the jeep. It felt good to be outside, ready for action.

Don led the way through the wood with a torch. The path wound downwards towards the loch. The water shimmered ahead of them through the trees. For once the mist on the moor had lifted; the night was clear and sharp and the moonlight strong. Atticus felt the same sense of belonging as he had when he first arrived on the moor. The landscape held a strange fascination for him. The scale of the place and its sheer emptiness were something he had never experienced before. The idea of being free to roam was enticing. He could

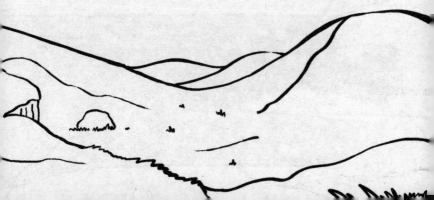

see why the wildcats valued their freedom so highly.

The path came to an end in a steep bank. Don scrambled down it and held out his hand to help the others. Atticus made his way sure-footed down the bank. He found himself on a shingle beach. Biggnaherry Castle was ahead and to the right on the hillside beyond the woods. Atticus hadn't seen the back of the castle before. It loomed above him, granite-faced and forbidding. Steps led from a wide patio into a sloping garden, which was separated from the beach at the bottom by a continuation of the steep bank. An uneven row of tall oak trees threaded its way along the perimeter. It was interspersed with tree stumps and tangled shrubs.

'According to the map, the entrance to the secret tunnel lies somewhere along there,' Mrs Tucker said, pointing to the bank beneath the oak trees. 'Don, can you give us the lie of the land? What's that room there?' She gestured at the big bay windows fronting the patio.

'That's the library,' Don explained. 'Lady Jemima doesn't use it very often. You can also get to the garden from the cellar beneath the kitchen. The door comes out in the well.'

Atticus looked carefully at the base of the steps. The steps ended in a paved well. He couldn't see the cellar door – it was concealed by shadows.

'My guess is that's where Lady Jemima lets the panther out,' Mrs Tucker said. She pointed along the beach. A dilapidated wooden hut stood adjacent to the water, a little distance from the bank. 'Is that the boathouse?'

'Yes.'

'Right, we'll pace out the tunnel entrance from there.'

'Sheeeeeeeeeeee!' Atticus's ears pricked up. The noise was coming from inside the boathouse.

'What was that?' asked Callie in alarm.

'Sheeeeeeeeeeee!' It came again.

Atticus knew what it was. The wildcat! Peregrine had caught it, just as he feared. The bird must be keeping it prisoner in the boathouse until it gave him the information he wanted. Atticus crept forwards on his belly.

'Atticus!' Mrs Tucker called sharply.

Atticus paid no attention.

'I'm going to get him,' said Michael.

'No,' Mrs Tucker said firmly. 'It's too dangerous. It might be the panther. Let's lie low for a minute until we're sure.'

The treasure hunters hid in the shadow of the bank.

Atticus had reached the boathouse. The decrepit planks were full of cracks. He put his eye to one of them and looked inside. His heart lurched.

A wildcat lay on the floor. Atticus recognised it at once. It was the same wildcat that had saved him from the panther the night before. It had the same beautiful markings, the same beautiful eyes. Its paws were tied together with rope. A net had been thrown into a corner, as had a large number of straps and some woolly socks full of thistles.

Atticus didn't have time to work out what they were doing there; all his attention was focused on the wildcat and its captors. There were nine of them altogether, standing in a circle around the stricken animal. He blinked. One of the birds looked remarkably familiar. He had glossy black-and-white feathers with a hint of blue about his wings, a touch of green on his tail and cruel, glittering eyes . . .

Jimmy Magpie!

Atticus could scarcely believe it. Peregrine he had expected. And the presence of seven of his creepy crow sidekicks came as no particular surprise. *But Jimmy Magpie?* Atticus hadn't seen that coming. He would think twice about leaving Jimmy all alone in Littleton-on-Sea without police surveillance next Christmas time.

But where were Thug and Slasher? Atticus's eyes scoured the boathouse. There was no sign of the other two magpies. They must be around somewhere, though. Jimmy never went anywhere without his gang.

Peregrine addressed the wildcat in his horrible screech. 'You know what we want,' he screamed.

'We can do this the easy way or the hard way . . .' He thrust his hooked beak towards the wildcat's face.

'Sheeeeeeeeee!' the wildcat spat at him.

Peregrine raised his mighty talons.

Atticus couldn't contain himself any longer. The wildcat had saved him, now it was his turn to save her. He wriggled through a hole in the bottom of the planks and launched himself at Peregrine.

Atticus had the initial advantage against the powerful falcon but Peregrine fought back fiercely. He lunged at Atticus with his sharp beak. Atticus dodged. He tried to pin the falcon by its tail but the bird twisted round and beat at Atticus with his strong wings.

'Get him!' screeched Peregrine.

The other birds surrounded Atticus. He was trapped.

'Well, well, well,' gloated Jimmy Magpie. 'Look who's here! I wish the boys could see this. Maybe Thug will get his furry nest snuggler after all.'

Atticus snarled. 'I hope he chokes on it,' he said.

Suddenly the door to the boathouse flew open. A disgusting smell of socks filled the hut.

'Not so fast, beak-face!'

It was Inspector Cheddar! Atticus had never before been so pleased to see the Inspector in his life, even if he did smell like he'd been rolling in mouldy Camembert.

The smell was truly disgusting. The birds coughed and spluttered. Peregrine doubled over, gasping for air. The wildcat twisted and bucked.

Atticus's eyes watered. He pulled his handkerchief over his nose and gave a strangled meow.

'Oh, you're there, Atticus!' Inspector Cheddar said, seeing him for the first time. 'Sorry about the smell. It's Thumpers' Cat Repellent. I borrowed it from Great-Uncle Archie in case I bumped into the Cat Sith.' He looked puzzled. 'Wait a minute, if you're Atticus, who's this, then?' He pointed to the wildcat.

Peregrine had partially recovered from the smell. Inspector Cheddar's moment of confusion over the two cats gave the falcon the chance he wanted. He flew at Inspector Cheddar, his eyes blazing with anger.

'SCCCCCRRRRREEEECCCCCCHHHHH!'

'Oh no you don't, you blasted bird!' Inspector Cheddar held up the frying pan.

BASH! Peregrine whammed straight into it, knocking himself out.

Mimi appeared at the door. Bones was just behind her.

'Cover your noses!' Atticus shouted.

The two cats put paws to their faces.

'Bones, you free the wildcat. Mimi, help me with this.' He held up the net in his paws.

Mimi took the other end in her free paw. Together they threw it over Peregrine's lieutenants who were still doubled over, choking. Atticus counted them up. There were only seven birds. 'Where's Jimmy?' he asked.

'Jimmy?' Mimi echoed. 'You mean Jimmy Magpie?'

Atticus nodded. 'He was here a minute ago, I swear. He must have escaped.'

'He can't cause any more trouble,' Mimi reassured him. 'Not with Peregrine out of the way.'

Atticus wished he could be so sure.

Inspector Cheddar shovelled Peregrine into the frying pan with the spatula and placed him under the net with the other birds. 'You're under arrest,' he said to them (although Peregrine didn't hear because he was still unconscious). 'It's a spell in Her Majesty's Prison for Bad Birds for you! Finish off in here, would you, Atticus? I think I need some fresh air.' Inspector Cheddar stepped outside.

'Shhhhheeeeeeeee!' The wildcat was still struggling.

'I can't untie you if you won't stay still,' Bones said in frustration. Bones was normally brilliant at tying and untying knots but every time she loosened the bungee ropes, the thrashings of the wildcat made them tight again.

'It's okay,' said Atticus soothingly. 'We won't hurt you. We want to help.'

The wildcat glanced at Atticus. Her body relaxed a little, although her breath came in rapid pants. Quickly Bones finished untying the knots. The wildcat shook off the ropes. She faced the three cats, her ears flat to her head.

'Sheeeeeeeee!' she hissed.

'What's wrong with her?' asked Mimi.

'She's scared,' Atticus said. He took a cautious step towards the wildcat. 'We want to help,' he said again. 'We know about Lady Jemima and the treasure. We know the sightings of the Cat Sith are nothing to do with you. Trust me, all we want is to stop Lady Jemima from spoiling the moor.'

The wildcat looked as if she was about to speak when a shrill voice came from outside the boathouse. 'Well, *hello*!' it said. 'If it isn't my long-lost cousin, two hundred times removed, Ian Larry Barry *Dumpling* Cheddar!'

'Oh no!' said Mimi. 'It's her!'

'Lady Jemima!' shouted Inspector Cheddar joyfully. 'You're safe!'

'Well, you're not,' said Lady Jemima. 'And neither is the rest of your rotten family and their revolting friends.' She sneezed loudly. 'And by the way, what is that horrible smell?'

Atticus peeped through the crack in the planks. His ears drooped. Lady Jemima Dumpling stood on the shingle beach in an old fur coat. In one hand she held a rusty pistol, in the other, the plastic folder containing the treasure map.

Lady Jemima gave a whistle. 'Bring them out, Chomper,' she said, 'to show Ian Larry Barry.'

From out of the shadows shuffled Callie, Michael, Mr and Mrs Tucker, Mrs Cheddar and Don and Debs. They were followed by the panther.

Atticus watched in horror. Lady Jemima had captured the treasure hunters.

Lady Jemima gave another whistle. The big black cat came to heel by her feet.

Inspector Cheddar looked stunned. 'I don't get

it,' he said, regarding the panther fearfully. 'Aren't you scared it's going to eat you?'

'There's no such thing as the Cat Sith, Dad!' Callie cried. 'The creature on the moor is Lady Jemima's pet panther. That's what you and Michael saw, not the Cat Sith.'

Callie had her left hand up, as though she was asking a question at school; her wrist twisted in the direction of Lady Jemima. Atticus wondered what she was doing. Then he caught a glimpse of her watch. *Of course!* Callie was wearing the spy watch that Mrs Tucker had given her for Christmas. She was recording everything.

'She sent it to scare you away in case you discovered she was after the treasure,' Callie told her dad. 'She wants to use it to turn the moor into a bingo park.'

'Do you?' Inspector Cheddar asked Lady Jemima, astonished.

'Yes,' replied Lady Jemima, 'I do, you silly fool. Everything she says is true.' She waved the treasure map at him. 'And now I've got Daddy's treasure map, it turns out Peregrine and his gang didn't need to catnap a wildcat after all.'

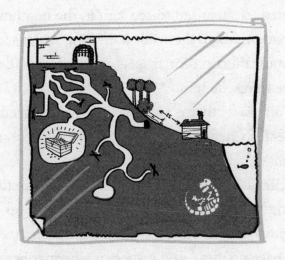

'So that's what those pesky birds were doing,' Inspector Cheddar muttered. 'I knew they were up to no good.'

'What does he mean?' Atticus whispered to Mimi.

'He must have witnessed the catnapping,' Mimi whispered back. 'And decided to come to the rescue.'

'But why would he do that?' Atticus wondered aloud.

'Maybe he thought the wildcat was you?' Bones guessed.

Of course! That's why Inspector Cheddar had

seemed so surprised to see him in the boathouse. He had mistaken the wildcat for him! Atticus felt a glow of affection for Inspector Cheddar. He had come to rescue him.

'You saw them?' Lady Jemima glanced at Inspector Cheddar shrewdly. 'So where's Peregrine now?'

Atticus tensed. If Lady Jemima found them hiding in the boathouse standing guard over her precious falcon, she'd set Chomper on them.

'I have no idea,' said Inspector Cheddar bravely.

Atticus was touched. Inspector Cheddar never ever lied. It was one of his golden rules. But he'd done it this time to protect the cats. Luckily Lady Jemima didn't seem to notice that Inspector Cheddar's face had gone a guilty shade of beetroot.

Instead she shrugged. 'He'll turn up at some point, I suppose.'

'What are you going to do with us?' Mrs Tucker demanded.

'Leave you somewhere in the cellars,' said Lady Jemima promptly. 'Meanwhile I shall blast the roof off the treasure chamber with dynamite, remove the gold through the kitchen and get the builders to start on Monday. If you manage to find a way out by then, I shall tell people you got lost trying to steal my gold and have you arrested; if you don't, you'll become part of the foundations for the new bingo park.'

'You fiend!' said Inspector Cheddar. 'I expected more of a Dumpling.'

Lady Jemima gave him a filthy look. 'Life's a gamble,' she said. 'I won. You lost. Now pace it out.' She consulted the map. 'It's twenty-five steps from the boathouse.'

'Or what?'

'I'll shoot you.'

'One, two, three, four . . .'

Inspector Cheddar did as he was told.

The others followed, Lady Jemima and Chomper bringing up the rear.

'GRRRRRRRRRR . . .' Luckily the stink coming from Inspector Cheddar seemed to have affected the panther's sense of smell. It walked past the boathouse without catching the scent of the cats hiding inside.

But Lady Jemima hadn't forgotten about them. 'By the way, where are those cats of yours?' Her voice drifted back on the breeze.

'Er . . .' said Inspector Cheddar.

Oh no! thought Atticus. *He can't tell two lies in a row.*

'They got lost,' Michael said quickly. 'On the moor.'

'Good,' said Lady Jemima.

'Psssssssst!' A soft voice behind him made Atticus jump. The wildcat was at his shoulder. 'Follow them,' she said. 'I'll go and get help.'

'Who from?' asked Atticus.

'The clan,' the wildcat replied. And with a flip of her tail she was gone.

Meanwhile, in the cellar under the kitchen . . .

Thug and Slasher were having an even worse time than the horrible time they'd been having since they first arrived at the Crow Brigade Army Training Camp.

Being stuck in a cellar underneath Biggnaherry Castle with a crew of belching, coughing, knuckle-cracking, dirty-joke-telling, farting, fight-picking, feather-pecking members of the Corvus family made the workout on the slippery rock, the early-morning swim in the freezing-cold loch and the rub-down with the prickly sock seem like a fun day out.

The rest of the birds were waiting for payment for their part in Peregrine's knockout Plan B. Only Thug and Slasher knew the truth about what was going to happen to them. But Jimmy had told them to hold off spilling the beans until he gave the word. And Thug and Slasher always did what their boss told them.

'I don't remember signing up for this,' Thug complained bitterly as a large jackdaw sat on his tail and passed wind.

'Me neither,' said Slasher, as a raven burped in

his face. 'If I don't get out of this dump in a minute I'll go mad.'

Thug managed a chuckle. ''Ere, Slash, you know what that will make you, don't you?'

'No, what?'

'A MAD-pie. Get it?' Thug punched him on the wing. 'Ha ha!'

'Ha ha!' Slasher punched him back.

'Chaka-chaka-chaka-chaka-chaka!'

'Chaka-chacka-chaka-chaka-chaka!'

As was usual at times of stress, the two magpies (or should it be mad-pies?) fell to squabbling.

'Stop it, you two!'

Thug and Slasher looked up.

The cellar had a little window high up in the wall. The window was fitted with bars. It was between these that Jimmy Magpie's face now appeared.

'Jimmy!' Thug cried. He fluttered up to the narrow ledge and took a gulp of fresh air.

'Do you know where the treasure is yet, Boss?' Slasher landed on the ledge beside Thug.

'Not quite yet,' Jimmy admitted.

'How come?' Thug asked in bewilderment.

'Because Peregrine's knockout Plan B just got

knocked out,' said Jimmy sourly. 'By Atticus Claw and that cheesy Inspector friend of his.'

'Claw?!' Slasher gasped. 'What's he doing here?'

'It turns out Inspector Cheese is a Dumpling,' Jimmy told him. He shook his head in disbelief. 'Looks like we've got competition, boys; Claw and his cronies are after the treasure too.'

'No way!'

'Yeah.' Jimmy quickly told them about the treasure map and how Lady Jemima was holding the other treasure hunters captive at gunpoint. 'Only none of them have reckoned on the Crow Brigade.' He tapped at the bars. 'We'll get everyone out through here.'

The window looked out into the well at the back of the castle where the stone steps finished.

'Prepare for mutiny, boys.' He jerked his head towards the waiting birds. 'It's time to tell your army pals what Peregrine and his boss really have planned for them.'

'Chaka-chaka-chaka-chaka-chaka!'

Thug and Slasher flew down and began to spread the word.

26

The entrance to the secret tunnel was concealed in the bank behind some twisted tree roots and thick clumps of grass. Without Stewart Dumpling's map, Atticus thought, it would have remained hidden from the humans forever.

'After you,' Lady Jemima said, waving the pistol.

The humans crawled into the tunnel, two abreast.

Atticus, Mimi and Bones crept cautiously along behind them. They couldn't risk getting too close in case Chomper saw them but equally they couldn't fall too far behind for fear of getting lost.

Atticus felt claustrophobic. The secret tunnel was damp. It was also extremely smelly, mainly thanks to Inspector Cheddar and Great-Uncle

Archie's cat repellent. Very soon they reached a junction where the tunnel divided into three. Not long after that they came across another junction where the tunnel divided again, then another and another. A maze was one way to describe the system of cellars; a rabbit warren was another. It was as complicated as the diagram of Inspector Cheddar's family tree. Even with the help of the treasure map, the leading group was having trouble. They only had torches to guide them, not sharp see-in-the-dark eyes like the cats did.

Atticus wished the wildcats would come. From time to time he thought he heard the brush of paws, but when he looked back he couldn't see anything. Maybe he was imagining things. Maybe the wildcats weren't coming after all. Maybe his friend from the moor had just promised to gather the clan so that she could get away.

'Don't worry, Atticus,' Mimi whispered, as though reading his thoughts. 'She won't let you down. She trusted you. You should trust her.'

Lady Jemima's voice interrupted Atticus's thoughts. 'Hooray!' she cried. 'We made it.' They had reached the chamber where the treasure was buried.

The three cats peeped into the room. The chamber had been carved out of the earth. The walls and floor were bare. Atticus imagined Domplagan sitting on his own on the dirt floor counting the Roman money, planning how he was going to spend it.

'We must be right under the castle,' Bones guessed aloud.

The humans had gathered around a great flagstone in the middle of the floor. Chomper stood outside the circle, pawing the ground impatiently.

'Open it,' Lady Jemima said to Debs.

Debs gave her a dirty look.

'Do it!' hissed Lady Jemima, fingering the trigger. 'Or Don's sporran is toast.'

Debs took hold of the flagstone and slid it to one side.

'Shine the light inside,' ordered Lady Jemima.

Don pointed his torch at the hole in the ground. The chamber was filled with a warm yellow glow, 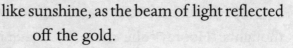 like sunshine, as the beam of light reflected off the gold.

226

'Finally!' Lady Jemima dropped to her knees and peered over the edge of the hole. 'It's mine!' she cried, picking up great handfuls of coins and letting them trickle through her fingers. 'Mine! Mine! Mine! Biggnaherry Bingo Park, here we come!'

Lady Jemima seemed to Atticus to be overwhelmed with greed. It was horrible to watch. No wonder the wildcats wanted to stop any of Domplagan's descendants getting their hands on the gold, he thought. They were all the same: as soon as they saw it they became mean and nasty and corrupt. Maybe even Lord Stewart wouldn't have kept his word about turning the moor into a sanctuary for the wildcats. Who knew what would actually have happened if he hadn't drowned in the loch?

'It's not yours,' Michael shouted at Lady Jemima. 'You're a crook. If it belongs to anyone, it's Dad's. He'll be next in line to the Dumpling fortune once you're in prison.'

This thought didn't seem to have occurred to Inspector Cheddar before. Suddenly his eyes took on a greedy, cunning expression. His face was bathed in golden light as he leant over the pit next to Lady Jemima, his eyes fixed on the treasure.

'Mine . . .' he whispered.

Oh no! Atticus thought. Now it was happening to *him* too!

'Darling, what on earth is wrong with you?' asked Mrs Cheddar in alarm.

'It must be the Dumpling in him,' Mrs Tucker hissed. 'As soon as they get a whiff of the gold they go crazy.'

'I knew this would happen,' Lady Jemima screamed. 'Chomper! Get him!'

Chomper stalked towards Inspector Cheddar. The Inspector leapt to his feet. 'Here, kitty, kitty,' he purred, extracting something from his pocket.

'Do you think we should help him?' asked Bones uncertainly.

'Definitely not,' said Atticus, squinting at the label. 'Hold your noses, everybody!'

'Grrrrrr!' The panther pounced.

Inspector Cheddar shook the box. An avalanche of white powder covered Chomper's black fur.

228

The panther ran for cover along one of the tunnels, whimpering.

Lady Jemima coughed and spluttered. Face filler streamed out of her ears. 'Will someone please tell me what that awful smell is?'

'Thumpers' Traditional Cat Repellent,' said Inspector Cheddar. He knocked the gun out of her hand with a quick karate chop and kicked it to the side of the chamber. 'Do you give up yet?'

'Never!' Lady Jemima's hands closed round Inspector Cheddar's throat. 'It's *my* gold!' she screamed.

'No, it's not, you greedy witch, it's *my* gold!' Inspector Cheddar closed his hands round Lady Jemima's throat.

The two of them toppled into the pit.

'No, it's not!' An angry chattering rang round the chamber. 'It's ours.'

Jimmy Magpie flew into the chamber with Thug and Slasher. They were followed by a great flock of angry birds. They swooped towards the gold.

'Watch out, everyone!' Mrs Tucker shouted as the birds filled the chamber. 'The magpies and their mates are back. Don't let them peck you.'

The humans crouched down, their hands covering their heads as the birds flapped and squawked.

'Oh dear,' said Mimi. 'Now what are we going to do?'

'Don't youze have something to scare them off with, Edna?' Mr Tucker roared.

Mrs Tucker normally carried useful gadgets in her basket, just in case.

'It's Christmas,' Mrs Tucker said. 'I'm supposed to be on holiday.'

'Wait, I've got an idea!' Michael said. 'Mum's lipstick! The one you gave her as a present!'

'Oh yes,' said Mrs Cheddar. 'I've got it somewhere.' She searched about in her pockets. 'Here.' She handed it to Mrs Tucker.

'Take cover, everyone!' Mrs Tucker took off the cap and pointed the lipstick towards the flock of birds.

Atticus, Mimi and Bones threw themselves to the floor.

BOOM!

A bright white firework fizzed out of the lipstick and exploded in a fountain of tiny stars.

'We're under attack!' screeched Jimmy.

'Let's get out of here!' screamed Slasher.

'Mayday! Mayday! Mayday!' One of Thug's tail feathers was on fire.

The three birds fled back down the tunnel, followed by the rest of the Crow Brigade.

'Chaka-chaka-chaka-chaka-chaka!'

Their chattering receded down the tunnel. It was met by a familiar hiss.

'Shhheeeeeeeeee!'

'Shhheeeeeeeeee!'

'Shhheeeeeeeeee!'

'Shhheeeeeeeeee!'

The wildcats. Atticus raised his head. They *had* come, after all. The beautiful cat from the moor stood beside him. Others gathered behind, at the entrance to the tunnel.

'Look!' Michael said in awe.

'The wildcats have made friends with Atticus,' said Callie. She held out her hand.

'Don't, Callie,' Don warned. 'They're not pets; they're wild.'

The humans stood stock-still.

The wildcat looked impassively at the scene before her. The birds had gone, but Inspector Cheddar and Lady Jemima were still fighting fiercely over the treasure in the pit. 'It is as we feared,' the wildcat hissed. 'The Roman gold always brings trouble. We must scare the humans away. Then we must hide the gold again, in a place that no one will ever find it.'

She flattened her ears and took a step towards the pit.

The other wildcats followed her lead. 'Shhheeeeeee! Shhheeeeeee! Shhheeeeeee!' they spat.

Atticus felt alarmed. It was only Lady Jemima who needed frightening away, not Inspector Cheddar! Or at least it would be if he stopped behaving like a greedy Dumpling.

'They won't hurt Dad, will they, Mum?' Callie said in a frightened voice.

'I don't think so,' Mrs Cheddar said.

Atticus wasn't so sure. The wildcats were just that: wild. And they believed they were fighting for their lives.

232

'No!' Atticus leapt in front of the wildcats.

The hissing stopped. The leader of the wildcats narrowed her eyes. 'I thought you were on our side,' she snarled.

'I am,' Atticus replied. 'I promise.' Mrs Cheddar's exploding lipstick had given him an idea. 'I think I know a way to end this forever, without anyone getting harmed.' Everyone else had used their Christmas presents, except him. Maybe his would work on Inspector Cheddar. 'Please!' he said. 'Just give me a few minutes.'

'Very well,' the leader of the wildcats agreed.

The other wildcats stirred restlessly behind her. He didn't have long.

Atticus raced over to where Callie and Michael huddled with their mum and Mrs Tucker.

'Atticus!' Callie gave him a big hug.

Atticus shook her off. He didn't want to look soppy in front of the wildcats. He had to look as if he was in charge. His police-cat badge was pinned to his handkerchief. He pawed at it impatiently. 'Meow!' he fretted.

'You want us to take it off?' Michael guessed. 'But why?'

Atticus pawed at it again. He didn't have time to explain now.

'Do what he wants, Michael,' Mrs Tucker said.

'Okay,' said Michael. 'Here.' Carefully he unpinned Atticus's police-cat-sergeant badge and laid it on the dirt floor.

Atticus picked it up in his teeth. Then, being careful that the pin didn't prick his mouth, he leapt into the treasure pit.

'Mine!'

'Mine!'

'Mine!'

'Mine!'

'Mine!'

'Mine!'

'Mine!'

'Mine!'

Lady Jemima and Inspector Cheddar were pelting one another with gold coins. They barely noticed Atticus.

Greed really was a terrible sin, thought Atticus fleetingly. He vowed never to be greedy again (except when it came to sardines and smokies, which didn't count). He took the badge in his paw and jabbed Inspector Cheddar hard in the arm with the pin.

'Get off!' shouted Inspector Cheddar, swiping at Atticus.

Atticus jabbed him again.

'What is it?' shouted Inspector Cheddar.

Atticus jabbed him again.

'Can't you see I'm busy?'

Atticus kept jabbing.

Inspector Cheddar grabbed the badge from Atticus. 'Mine!' he shouted in delight. 'Mine! Mine! Mine! Mine! Mine! Mine! Mine! Mine!' He held it up to the light. Atticus's police-cat badge twinkled back at him brightly. In fact it was much brighter than the mountain of golden coins Inspector Cheddar was perched on because Atticus had been polishing it every morning with the Badge Bright the Inspector had given him for Christmas.

Suddenly Inspector Cheddar realised what it was. 'Oh,' he said. He looked at the bedraggled figure of Lady Jemima. 'Ah,' he said. He looked up at the anxious faces staring down at him from the edge of the pit. 'I see what you mean,' he said. 'I'm being an awful chump, aren't I?'

Everyone nodded.

Inspector Cheddar gathered himself. 'Thank you, Atticus,' he said. He gave the police-cat badge back to Atticus, emptied his pockets of gold coins and turned back to Lady Jemima. Then he assumed his most policeman-like expression. 'You're under arrest,' he said, producing a pair of handcuffs from somewhere and clamping them round Lady Jemima's wrists.

'Noooooo!' she screamed.

'You have a right to remain silent, but anything you do say will be taken down and may be used in evidence against you,' Inspector Cheddar continued. 'Except "knickers".'

'This is all *your* fault.' Lady Jemima glowered at Atticus. 'I knew you were tricky.'

Tricky was one way of putting it; world's greatest cat detective was another. Atticus gave her a parting growl and leapt out of the pit with the Inspector.

The wildcats had retreated to the tunnel entrance but they were still watching the Inspector closely.

'I recorded everything, Dad,' Callie

236

said, tapping her watch. 'Lady Jemima's definitely going to prison.'

'Well done, Callie,' Inspector Cheddar said proudly. 'You'll make a brilliant detective one day.'

'This means you'll inherit the gold, Dad,' Michael reminded him.

Inspector Cheddar smiled ruefully. 'I don't think I want it after all,' he said, glancing gratefully at Atticus.

'But what are you going to do with it, then?' asked Mrs Cheddar.

'We've got an idea,' Callie said, smiling broadly at her brother.

'What?' said Inspector Cheddar.

Michael was smiling too.

Atticus crossed his paws.

'You can use it to turn the moor into a wildcat sanctuary!'

Inspector Cheddar gave them both a big hug. 'That's exactly what I'll do,' he said. 'What a good idea!'

Atticus watched the three of them affectionately. Inspector Cheddar wasn't all that bad, really, once you got to know him. And the kids and Mrs Cheddar loved him, which counted for a lot.

'You did it, Atticus!' Mimi and Bones congratulated him. 'You saved the moor!'

'We all did,' Atticus said modestly. 'Not just me.' He looked around for the wildcats so that he could say goodbye, but they had already melted away into the maze of tunnels and disappeared.

27.

It was New Year's Eve and at Biggnaherry Castle the Hogmanay party was in full swing. Everyone had come from the village by bus to celebrate.

Chomper had been rounded up by a team from a nearby safari park and taken to live there. No one was scared of the Cat Sith any more, not now the moor was to be turned into a wildlife sanctuary and the wildcats were finally safe.

Even Great-Uncle Archie had been persuaded out of his room for the night to join in the celebrations. And, now that he knew that the Cat Sith wasn't real, Great-Uncle Archie wasn't so frightened of *ordinary* cats any more. He and Mr Tucker sat in the drawing room, smoking smokie pipes and telling each other scary stories. Bones sat between them contentedly, practising knots with a piece of string.

Atticus and Mimi were in the kitchen eating delicious scraps of party food. They were waiting for the final game of the evening to take place. So far, Debs had won everything except the hairiest sporran competition, which had gone to Don, and the wrestling, which had been won by Mrs Tucker. (Mrs Cheddar had cancelled the skinny-dip in the loch, in case anyone got cramp and drowned like poor old Stewart Dumpling.)

'Would all the competitors for the final event please make their way to the library,' Mrs Cheddar announced through a megaphone. 'The cheese throwing will take place from the patio.'

Atticus and Mimi followed the excited crowd of people into the library. It was a lovely room lined from floor to ceiling with shelves crammed with dusty books. He was glad it was going to be

240

preserved, along with the rest of the castle, which was to be turned into a visitors' centre for people who came to visit the wildcat sanctuary. Inspector Cheddar had asked Don and Debs if they would look after it and to everyone's delight they had agreed.

Mrs Cheddar ushered the crowd on to the patio. Inspector Cheddar took his place between Debs and Mrs Tucker. He had his cheese-throwing outfit on – a bright blue nylon tracksuit with his name stitched on the back. Lots of other people from the village were taking part too.

'On your marks . . .' Mrs Cheddar said.

The competitors selected their cheeses from a big pile in the middle of the patio.

'Get set . . .'

The competitors stood beside the patio wall and hefted the cheeses to their chins.

'Throw!'

The cheeses sailed into the air like cannonballs and landed in the floodlit garden. All except one, which landed with a splash in the loch.

'And the winner is my darling husband, Inspector

Ian Larry Barry Dumpling Cheddar!' Mrs Cheddar said, throwing her arms around him.

'Well done!' Debs said generously. 'That was the best cheese throw I've ever seen.' She handed him the trophy.

Everyone clapped Inspector Cheddar on the back. The happy crowd disappeared inside the library.

Atticus sat on the patio wall and gazed out over the loch. Beyond it lay the moor. Both were shrouded in mist. He wondered where the wildcats were. At least he'd learnt *something* about his past, he reflected. The way he felt about the moor, the way he looked, Don was right – he definitely must have some Highland Tiger in him somewhere along the line.

Mimi jumped up beside him.

'Do you want to join them?' she asked quietly. 'Only I'd understand, you know, if you did. History is a powerful thing. It gives you a sense of belonging.'

Atticus took a deep breath of the fresh, zingy air. He was glad to have met his distant cousins, the wildcats, but since he'd lived at Littleton-on-Sea with the Cheddars he already *had* a sense of belonging. 'Not really,' he said. 'I mean, I did think about it a bit, but it's not for me. I'd rather stay with you and the Cheddars. We're a family.'

'I'm glad,' Mimi said, squeezing his paw.

Atticus squeezed it back. His eyes gleamed in the moonlight. 'Besides,' he added mischievously, 'that way we can have some more adventures.'

Author's Note

Atticus Claw on the Misty Moor started life about ten years ago as *The Legend of the Loch*. It was the first book I had ever written and, fortunately for you, it never got published. The only good thing about it was the plot. I always felt a touch nostalgic about it though, so when I decided to set Atticus's sixth adventure in Scotland, I dug the manuscript out of a box, dusted it off and pulled out the best bits to use again. The original inspiration for the story was Rosemary Sutcliffe's wonderful book *The Eagle of the Ninth* about a legion of Roman soldiers which mysteriously disappeared in Caledonia in AD 117. All I can say is if you haven't already read it, I strongly recommend that you do!

I was sorry to say goodbye to all my new friends in Scotland, but I'm glad we saved the moor for the wildcats. Hopefully it won't be long before I have another adventure . . . They do seem to happen to me all the time!

'*Atticus Claw Breaks the Law* is now one of my all-time favourite books. It is un-put-down-able.'
Helen, age 10

'Atticus Claw is a masterpiece!'
Sam, age 12

'Very funny and interesting.'
Ara, age 9

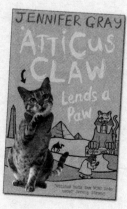